THE SURVIVALIST 8
THE END IS COMING

The Russians around  the
second tank already s
the Russians who had
tanks returned fire. T
hundred yards or so
the automatic weapo

Rourke felt a smile cross his lips ,
and he was up, the CAR–15's safety coming on
under his right thumb, raising his body from its
crouch, moving into a long-strided run toward the
Harley. There was a roar, a high-pitched loud
whistling sound – the 125mm smooth-bore turret gun.
He broke through the tree line, running, feeling the
ground tremble as he was slapped forward by a rush of
air – the HEAT round had impacted to the left of his
original line of movement.

If he hadn't broken right, he realised, looking back
through the cloud of smoke and dirt and foliage
raining down, he would have been dead . . .

*The Survivalist series by Jerry Ahern, published
by New English Library:*

THE SURVIVALIST 8 THE END IS COMING

Jerry Ahern

NEW ENGLISH LIBRARY

First published in the USA in 1984 by
Kensington Publishing Corporation

First NEL Paperback Edition July 1985

NEL Books are published by
New English Library,
Mill Road, Dunton Green,
Sevenoaks, Kent.
Editorial office: 47 Bedford Square, London WC1B 3DP

Printed and bound in Great Britain by
Cox & Wyman Ltd, Reading.

British Library C.I.P.

Ahern, Jerry
  The survivalist.
  8: The end is coming
  I. Title
  813′.54[F]   PS3551.H4/

  ISBN 0–450–05830–1

For the readers who've called and written—asked, "When will Rourke find his wife and children?" This one's for you—

Chapter One

Rourke eased the dead Mulliner boy's head to the rocks. Rourke stood up, tired suddenly, more tired than he had been for so long he couldn't remember.

He walked the few paces to the stream at the base of the falls, the roar there loud, steady, throbbing, pulsing in his ears. Spray pelted at his face as he dropped to his knees beside the water, dipping his right hand down, moving his fingers slowly in the cold, roaring waters, the blood drifting from them—Bill Mulliner's blood—forming clouds in the water, red.

He heard movement behind him. He knew the source. Rourke closed his eyes, felt the hands—soft, cool—touch at his neck, move across his face.

"You have found them, John—"

"Probably," Rourke answered, his voice soft, a whisper.

"I'll take Paul to the Retreat—he can help me to unload the cargo from the aircraft and we can get

7

it to the Retreat — I'll stay with him until you come back."

Rourke opened his eyes, hearing the water rushing, watching it move, turning his head, still on his knees, looking up at her. "And?"

"My uncle — I'll go back — to Chicago — to the KGB — to —"

Rourke stood up, the falls roaring now, as loudly as his blood in the veins at his temples roared, his heart fast. "No," he rasped, drawing her into his arms.

Natalia's hands — he felt them move across his face, into his hair, his arms bound tightly around her waist and shoulders. He looked at her, at her eyes, their blueness, the whiteness of her skin — her mouth, the lips moist, slightly parting as she leaned her face toward his.

Rourke bent his face, his lips touching lightly at hers, then crushing down against her mouth, her body pressed tight against him.

Her hands — he could feel them move, he could feel her breath on his skin, her body rising and falling against his, the pressure of her breasts against his chest.

Then her face was beside his, half against his left shoulder.

He heard himself telling her, "I love you — you won't leave — you won't go back —"

"Sarah," she whispered.

"I — I — I can't — I love her, too — I —"

"I'll leave —"

Rourke took Natalia's arms roughly in bunched fists, holding her away from him at arms' length, her face downturned, her hair falling forward, her body limp-seeming. "You won't leave me — I won't — I won't let —"

She looked up at him, her eyes open, wet at the rims, making their blueness that much more bright. Her left hand reached out to him, halting, awkward because of the way he held her upper arms below the shoulders. The fingers of her hand, splayed, now closed, soft as they touched against his lips. "I'll stay with you forever if you want me —"

Rourke drew her against him. "Yes," he whispered, not knowing what else to say. He laughed, and she looked up at his face.

"John?"

"I never planned for this," he said, holding her, hugging her against him, hearing the sound of the water and the sound of her breathing . . . .

Chapter Two

"Do you think, Paul—well—what do you think?" She looked at Rubenstein as they rode along the level grasslands to intersect the highway leading nearest to the Retreat. He didn't answer her—and she started to raise her voice over the throb of the Harleys' engines, to repeat her question. "Paul—I wanted to know—do you—"

She watched as he took his eyes from the path of the bikes, as his left hand moved slowly upward, pushing the wire-rimmed glasses off the bridge of his nose. "I heard you—I just didn't know what to answer you. I didn't know what to think—to say—I don't know—"

"You think I'm crazy?" And she slowed the Harley under her, arcing it in a wide circle in the grass of the gently rolling field, a house distantly visible, but no sign of human habitation beyond that, and no sign of occupancy. Rubenstein's bike slowed ahead of her, turning in a lazy circle back toward her, Natalia watching as the wind tossed his thinning hair, tossed the high, uncut grass as well, hearing the evenness of the Harley's engine. Then

10

the silence as the engine cut out, like her own had.

"What do you want me to say? That I think John should have two wives? Remember, Jews aren't polygamous. And neither are Russians, I hear—so I can't tell you anything more than you know yourself, Natalia."

"But—" She looked down at the controls of her machine—they were unchanging. She rested her hands on the flap coverings of her belt holsters, feeling the weight of the two L-Frame Smith & Wessons in the gunbelt at her hips. "I just—ahh—I don't—"

"John wants you to stay—and you want to stay. And for what it matters," and she watched his eyes behind his glasses. "For what it matters—well—I want you to stay, too—I do—" The background silence broke, Paul Rubenstein's Harley gunning to life. He just looked at her, Natalia hearing his voice above its throb. "Ready?"

She nodded to him—but it might have been a lie . . . .

She had insisted on using the road—crossing the rougher country was difficult with Paul's wound, difficult for him, pain etched more deeply across his face with each bump and twist. And the highway was faster as well. And it was only a few miles to ride. She had given herself all of these arguments and then given them to Paul—and Paul Rubenstein had relented.

A peacefulness had come about her now—the peacefulness that she had sometimes felt in her life when destiny was beyond her control. John Rourke would find his Sarah, and Michael, and

11

Annie. What would happen after that would happen. Rourke had ordered her to stay—and she would. Two men in her life she had felt merited her obedience—her uncle, General Ishmael Varakov, supreme commander of Soviet Forces of the North American Army of Occupation, and Doctor John Thomas Rourke—she rolled the name on her tongue.

When she had met and married Vladmir Karamatsov, she had thought she had fallen in love—but she had realized soon that she had been taken in. She was the niece of one of the Soviet Union's most highly placed military commanders, the Soviet Union's most respected soldier of World War II—and he was the hero of World War III, she knew, but his praises would never be sung. Rather than a bath of blood, he had sought to handle his task with as much equanimity as possible, to treat the conquered American people—she smiled at that, for Americans truly seemed unconquerable on the most fundamental of levels—to treat them like people, with dignity. To get his job done—the job of supplying the Soviet war effort in Asia against the Chinese Communists, but to restrain the KGB from its intended purge—had brought her uncle into conflict with her husband, and it was this conflict that had led to her husband's abuse of her body, of her soul—had led to her uncle's constructing events in such a way that John Rourke had no choice but to kill her husband.

Her Uncle Ishmael—she smiled at the thought. A humanist, a good humanist—and perhaps because of that, he was a better Communist than all of them.

And John Rourke—as dedicated an anti-Communist as she had ever known, as she had ever thought could exist, but capable of great tenderness, of love, of understanding. And she loved both men—the Communist general and the anti-Communist doctor and survivalist. And both men loved her. It was a happiness that she felt—despite the aftermath of global thermonuclear war. And the idea of happiness was itself ridiculous.

But Natalia Anastasia Tiemerovna, major, Committee for State Security of the Soviet, felt it—happiness—anyway.

She wanted to say something to Paul—that she loved him deeply like she would love a brother, or a close friend—she had had neither.

She turned her face, her hair caught in the slipstream of the air around her and the Harley that throbbed between her legs. She looked at Rubenstein as she brushed hair back from her eyes.

She felt stupid, shouting it to him. "I'm happy, Paul!"

They were starting into a curve as they passed beneath an outstretching roadside oak to their right, the angle of the road dropping steeply left, an abandoned roadside store on the left perhaps forty yards ahead. In the gravel parking lot between the store and the road were more than a dozen men on motorcycles or standing beside them. Heavily armed, the men were Brigands.

She swung her M-16 forward on its sling. She slowed her bike. She looked at Paul Rubenstein—

his German MP–40 submachine gun was in his right fist. She felt a tear at the inside corner of her right eye. Natalia Anastasia Tiemerovna, major, Committee for State Security of the Soviet, told herself the tear in her eye was only from the wind. It had been foolish — dangerous — to feel happy.

Chapter Three

He laughed when he thought of it — "trigger control." It had been his slogan, his watchword, so long — but so little time — ago. Paul Rubenstein pumped the Schmeisser's trigger, a neat three-round burst across the forty yards or so separating him and Natalia from the dozen Brigands, pumped the burst toward the nearest of the two Brigands raising assault rifles toward them. And the Brigand — a tall, beefy man wearing a sleeveless blue denim jacket — doubled up jacknife fashion, falling forward.

A sharper, louder crack, hot brass pelting at his left cheek — Natalia's M-16, a long burst, the second rifleman going down, his legs cut from under him, gunfire raining toward them now as others of the Brigand band opened fire, motorcycles starting out of the gravel parking lot, skidding into the loop of highway that flanked the lot on two sides.

"Back the other way!" Natalia was screaming. Rubenstein fired another burst, then another and another, the comparatively mild recoil shocking his body, bringing a wash of cold sweat to him, his arms aching like a bad tooth. He started cutting the Harley into a steep arc, firing another burst, downing still another of the Brigand bikers, the Brigand's machine—a Japanese bike dripping chrome and gleaming like something just off a showroom floor—skidding across the highway. The Brigand was screaming, dragged behind it, the bike's engine roaring, sparks showering up from the road surface, then a scream more hideous than anything Paul Rubenstein had ever heard—a shriek. The Brigand's left leg, as the machine whiplashed against a rock of massive proportions, the rock a barrier between the corner of the gravel lot and the loop of highway—the left leg was torn away, the bike exploding as it struck the boulder-sized rock, a spray of flaming gasoline belching laterally across the loop of highway then rising, the amputated leg of the Brigand like a flaming log, the Brigand himself screaming again as flames engulfed his thrashing body.

Rubenstein fired out the Schmeisser's magazine through the sheet of flame, a Brigand biker crashing through it, bouncing to the highway, clothes and hair and face on fire.

Rubenstein let the Schmeisser drop to his side on its sling, snatching the battered Browning High Power from the web tanker style shoulder rig under his field jacket, jacking back the hammer with his thumb. He fired once—the Brigand biker, a human torch, dropped, the burning arms and hands slapping up toward the face, the face like the burning head of a match. What had been a man fell.

16

Rubenstein gunned the Harley, Natalia twenty yards back along the road by now, her machine stopped, the M-16 held in both her hands as she twisted in the bike seat, spraying death behind them.

He shouted to her over the crackle of flames and gunfire — "Run for it!"

He shot his machine past her, hearing her machine rev on the whistle of the slipstream.

Paul Rubenstein looked behind him — Natalia was coming, riding low over her Harley, Brigand bikers — at least six of them — starting out of the loop of highway and following.

Chapter Four

The M–16's thirty-round magazine spent, she let the rifle fall on its sling, dismissing it as she leaned her weight forward over the Harley, tucking her body down against the gunfire of the pursuing Brigands.

Paul Rubenstein was ahead of her, his machine weaving — perhaps to avoid Brigand gunfire, perhaps the pain in his arm making him weak. She didn't know.

Natalia kept riding.

There was a roar behind her and she looked back.

One of the Brigand bikers — he was breaking away from the rest, a three-wheeled trike, the roar of its engine loud. She stared at the machine. From what she could tell it was no real bike at all — something customized, hand built, chrome pipes gleaming everywhere, a chrome-plated auto-mobile-sized engine between the single front wheel and the rear wheels, just behind the driver's seat. There was a rippling, exploding sound, the bike up on its rear wheels for an instant, then rocketing toward her, a cloud of exhaust fumes rising in its wake.

The face of the man driving it — lips wide back from the bared teeth, snarling, one eye gone, the right one. In the left hand she saw a shotgun, the barrels short, no buttstock at all, as far as she could see.

The double side-by-side barrels were raising toward her as the three-wheeled machine gained on her.

Natalia reached her right hand to the Safariland flap holster at her right hip, her fingers curling around the smooth, memory-grooved Goncalo Alves stocks, the L-Frame Smith & Wesson in her fist as she wrenched it from the leather.

She punched the Metalife Custom .357 Magnum out, toward the man with the shotgun coming at her on the trike. If he fired first — she would be dead or worse, she knew. She double-actioned the slab-side barreled revolver, the wheelgun bucking in her right hand, the face of the Brigand biker seeming to erupt at the bridge of the nose and between the eyes. The shotgun discharged, both barrels, Natalia turning her face away, hearing a roar then a roar louder than the shotgun blasts had been, feeling heat sear at her right hand. She turned to fire again — but the trike, the biker, a massive oak tree growing close out of the side of the road — the bizarre machine had climbed it, hung from it now as flames rained down in chunks of burning flesh and debris and the trike and the biker who had ridden it were gone.

She holstered the L-Frame, one of two given her

19

by the de facto President of U.S. II, Samuel Chambers—in her mind's eye she could see the American Eagles engraved on the right barrel flats, remember the look in Rourke's eyes as Chambers had awarded her the guns, his token of thanks—

She was Russian, fighting Americans, fighting Russians, too, by hiding from them—at war with her own KGB—at war with her own heart.

Natalia screamed into the wind—

The Brigand bikers had given up their pursuit.

Chapter Five

Rourke slowed the jet-black Harley Low Rider. He eased the bike into a stop, letting down the stand, dismounting, sliding the CAR-15 forward on its sling.

He stood beside the Harley, listening. He could hear faint clicking sounds as the Harley's engine cooled, but, above these, he heard the sounds that had precipitated the Night of The War—the sounds of advancing Soviet tanks.

The CAR-15's pistol grip clenched tight in his right fist, he walked ahead, leaving the Harley by the side of the road—a dirt track leading from one main highway to another through farms and woods.

He entered the woods now, moving slowly, pushing aside overhanging branches, not breaking them, ducking the larger ones, squinting against the cool sunlight through his dark-lensed aviator-style sunglasses. He moved the short, dark tobacco cigar with his tongue from the right side of his mouth across his teeth to the left, clenching it there, still unlit.

The sound of the tanks was louder. He kept walking, the ground rising suddenly, dramatically ahead of him.

He slipped the rifle slightly further forward, its muzzle plug already pocketed, the lens caps for the Colt three-power scope already removed, pocketed in his brown leather bomber jacket like the muzzle cap.

His right thumb played against the Colt rifle's safety lever, the ball of his thumb rubbing against it, the safety off because there was no round in the CAR-15's chamber. Aboard a bike in rough country, it was safer to travel that way.

The tree cover thinned as the ground rose, Rourke stopping near its edge, listening.

Tanks — many tanks.

"Tanks a lot," he almost whispered, smiling at his own joke. He eared back the CAR-15's bolt, chambering the top round out of the thirty-round stick.

He chewed down harder on the cigar, flicking the safety to "on" and finding the Zippo in his Levis pocket. He flicked back the cowling, rolling the striking wheel under his thumb, poking the tip of the cigar into the blue-yellow flame. He eyed the initials on the old Zippo — J.T.R.

He pocketed the lighter.

Inhaling the smoke deep into his lungs, he walked from the tree line, glancing right and left and ahead, searching for anything that didn't belong as his ears focused the bulk of his attention on the sound of the tanks.

The ground was rising sharply now, and he

judged that he'd be able to view the tanks from the lip of the rise.

Rourke walked ahead, dropping into a crouch as he approached the height of the rise.

Chewing down on the cigar as he inhaled, he dropped onto his knees and elbows, raising his rifle into his fists as he moved on, then stopped. There was no need for binoculars, or even the scope on the CAR-15—at the distance of perhaps a quarter-mile, the ten tanks traveling in column along what had once been an interstate highway were visible enough. The tanks were thirty-nine plus ton T-72s, fitted with 125mm smooth-bore turret guns—more powerful than anything U.S. II might possibly have to throw against them.

The confidence of the tankers upset him most of all—they traveled with hatches up and open, heads and shoulders protruding above the hatches, men sitting on the tank bodies, hitching rides—Soviet soldiers.

As he watched, the tank column slowed, then stopped.

Rourke set down his rifle, snatching up his binoculars from the case at his side. He focused the armored Bushnell 8x30s on the head of the column. He could see no reason for the tanks to have stopped. He swept the binoculars forward, along the roadway.

An overpass bridge. In the shelter of the center pylons he saw something moving.

He focused the binoculars more sharply for the increased range.

A dog—a stray dog, like hundreds he had seen

since the Night of The War. Homeless, dirty, wild — ready to rip your throat to eat rather than starve. It looked part collie, perhaps part golden retriever — it was the right color for that. She was — as the dog began to stand up, he could make out beside it on the ground two puppies, barely visible. What the world desperately needed, he thought, were more stray dogs.

He swept his binoculars back to the lead tank, nearer to him than the dogs themselves, the road angling away from him in the direction in which the tanks moved.

The hatch open like the others, a man was clambering up and out of the hatch. There was an argument going on — between the man from the tank and one of the outside riders. The focal point of the argument seemed to be an AKM.

Rourke squinted, returned his gaze to the dogs. The female, the mother, was attempting to carry one pup by the scruff of the neck in her mouth, nudging the other pup with her forelegs, with her muzzle. She dropped the puppy from her mouth as she nudged at the other one. It rolled, unable to fully stand. She picked it up again, nudging at the other puppy once more.

Rourke heard the sound — automatic weapons fire.

The mother dog fell — a broad splotch of red suddenly visible on her neck behind her right ear. The puppy in her mouth was also shot — its body cut in half. Another burst of automatic weapons fire — the little puppy on the ground. Its body seemed almost to disintegrate.

Rourke swept the binoculars back to the lead tank — the man from inside the tank held the Soviet assault rifle to his shoulder, fired another burst, then handed the weapon back to the outside rider.

The man from the tank was laughing. Rourke could see him — laughing.

Rourke chewed down harder on his cigar, feeling the smoke in his lungs. He replaced the Bushnells in the pouch, zippered it shut.

He raised the CAR-15, extending the telescoped buttstock.

He judged the range at just under four hundred and fifty yards — stretching the CAR-15 beyond common sense and reason.

If he'd had the Steyr-Mannlicher SSG, twice the range would have been possible and easily so.

He settled the three-power scope's reticle — between the shoulder blades of the man from the lead tank, the man who had fired the AK.

Rourke closed his right eye a moment — he had killed wild dogs, many of them since the Night of The War.

What the tanker — the commander likely — had done was something altogether different, he realized.

And besides, Rourke thought — riding with the hatch open seemed to assume no American would fight back against the tanks, would resist the Soviet invaders.

Rourke moved the safety. He started the trigger squeeze.

He felt the recoil, heard the crack, saw the

scope shift slightly, blurred, then saw the man at the hatch of the lead tank, the man who had killed the dog and her two puppies—saw both hands move suddenly to the small of the back just above the belt, dead center over the spine. The body toppled forward, sliding across the front edge of the tank, slipping to the ground. The arms flapped once, twice—then no movement. Rourke made a mental note to experiment with bullet drop figures in excess of four hundred yards—he had aimed substantially higher.

As soon as he got the opportunity.

The Russians around the lead tank were moving, the second tank already starting laterally across the road—some of the Russians who had ridden on the outside of the tanks, now hidden beside the treads, returned fire. The rocks below Rourke and a hundred yards or so ahead of him took the impact of the automatic weapons fire.

Rourke felt a smile cross his lips. "So long, asshole," and he was up, moving, the CAR-15's safety coming on under his right thumb, raising his body up from its crouch, breaking into a long-strided run toward the Harley. There was a roar, a high-pitched loud whistling sound—the 125mm smooth-bore turret gun. He moved fast into a right angle, breaking through the tree line, running, feeling the ground tremble as he was slapped forward by a rush of air—the HEAT round had impacted to the left of his original line of movement. If he hadn't broken right, he realized, looking back through the cloud of smoke and dirt and foliage raining down, he would have been dead. Rourke pushed himself up, running again — if he could make the Harley, maximum speed on the T-72 series was fifty miles per hour — the Harley could do better than that — and effortlessly.

He kept running, but at an oblique angle now, to his left — the tank gunner would try to saturate the area. The gunner had fired left, now he would fire right — the whistling sound again, the roar of a blast dying on the air.

Rourke threw himself into the run, the whistling louder, higher pitched.

He hurtled himself forward through an opening in the tree cover, shielding his head with his hands. He felt the ground shake — but feeling at all meant he was still alive. Before the explosion died, he was up, running, a cloudburst of dust and broken bits of foliage engulfing the woods around him.

Fire — he looked behind him, the trees burning near the two impact sites.

He broke through the tree line — his bike, Soviet soldiers, six of them — they surrounded the machine, their own motorcycles parked on the opposite side of the dirt track.

The nearest of the men was turning, toward him.

No time for the CAR-15, Rourke's right hand flashed under his brown leather bomber jacket, snatching at the Pachmayr gripped butt of the stainless Detonics there. As the Soviet soldier raised his AKM, Rourke fired, the pistol bucking in his hand.

27

The soldier's face took the 185-grain JHP—the center of the face collapsing in the redness of blood as the man fell back.

A second soldier—Rourke shot him twice in the chest, Rourke's left arm going out, his left fist straight-arming a third soldier in the chest, knocking the man back and down.

Rourke jumped, his left leg snaking over the seat of the Harley Low Rider. He got the stand up, firing the Harley's engine, pumping the trigger of the Detonics into the chest and abdomen of a fourth Soviet soldier. The little Detonics was empty, the slide locked back. He thumbed down the stop, letting the slide run forward, ramming the pistol into his belt. A fifth Soviet soldier—Rourke's left leg snapped up and out, the toe of his combat-booted foot catching the man in the groin as the soldier tried to bring his rifle to bear. Rourke gunned the Harley, almost losing his balance, dragging his feet, keeping upright and taking off along the dirt road.

The Low Rider was best suited to highway driving, and making high speed on the bumpy, rutted dirt road was difficult, keeping it up harder—he let the machine out as much as he dared, keeping low over the handlebars as he looked back—one of the Soviet bikers was already coming, two more were mounting up.

Rourke's right hand slipped down to the CAR-15, his thumb working the safety off—he twisted the muzzle behind him, firing once, twice, a third time, the Soviet biker nearest him skidding off into the trees to avoid Rourke's fire. Rourke

28

worked the safety again, letting the CAR-15 drop on its sling at his side, his attention wholly focused now on riding.

Behind him, he could hear the sounds of bikes — the remaining two Soviets. He bent lower over the Harley — he made it there was at least another mile of the dirt track before he reached paved highway.

A deep rut — Rourke skirted the machine around it, balancing out with his feet, then gunning the engine, jumping a huge bump, wrenching the machine up with his arms, gunfire from behind him now. He looked back again — two bikers close, a third fifty yards or so behind them.

He couldn't risk firing, the road too rutted for him to shift a hand from the handlebars. His body low across the jet black Harley, he kept riding. There was a sharp bend right, Rourke's machine skidding through the curve, his right leg out, balancing the Harley, his right foot dragging through the mud as the road dipped, the Harley grinding, Rourke wrenching at the machine. Moving again — he kept the machine moving, through the curve and up the grade, the mud hard and rutted again, Rourke jumping the bike laterally over a deep rut, the machine skidding, Rourke balancing it out. Still moving.

A shouted curse from behind him — Rourke looked back, seeing one of the Soviet bikers down.

He gunned the Harley, taking the grade, jumping a hummock of ground, the dirt road evening out, Rourke letting out the machine—ahead he could see paved road.

A ridge of packed hard mud and gravel—he jumped the Harley over it, nearly losing it, recovering, letting the bike skid almost out from under him as he angled the machine right—he was on the road.

Balancing out, his feet up, he revved the Harley, the crackle of his exhaust loud, gunfire behind him as the coolness of the day turned into a chill slipstream around him, Rourke molding his body over the machine.

The road was a straight ribbon, black, recently paved, he guessed, before the Night of The War, the yellow double lines bright, fresh-painted.

Gunfire—the road surface behind him sparked with it as he looked back. Two of the Soviet bikers still pursued.

His exhaust rumbled, sputtered, made a sound that seemed to split the fabric of the air as he let the machine full out, the front wheel rising slightly, Rourke balancing as he fought the fork—and then the slipstream around him was harder, louder, colder, punching at his face, tearing at his hair—the gunfire was suddenly more distant.

He risked a look back once—the military bikes of the Soviet soldiers were fading in the distance.

He chewed down once, hard, on his cigar butt, then spit it into the slipstream.

Chapter Six

There had been more Russians as Rourke had moved off the highway and kept to the side roads, the dirt tracks—more and more Russians. Supply convoys—tanks riding shotgun for them—moved along each major artery in the directions of cities large enough to have airports. He had spent hours watching them, unable to move because of them, waiting.

A truck had broken down—an axle, Rourke had guessed, watching from the distance with his Bushnell 8x30s. After some time of Russian officers wandering about the truck, apparently shouting orders, cursing out the driver and the like, the truck had been unloaded.

Rourke had expected confiscated M-16s, or explosives, or foodstuffs—even medical supplies. But when one of the crates had broken—more stomping around, more apparent name-calling and threatening—the contents had proven to be a microfilm projector. All of the cases inside the truck—as they were emptied out with meticulous care—were apparently possessed of the same contents.

Rourke sat back, not looking at the road, considering instead.

He studied the CAR-15 as he laid it across his lap—how many thousands of rounds had he fired through it? The parkerized finish of the thirty-round magazine up the well was badly scratched, but the magazine was wholly serviceable. Absent-mindedly, he wondered if his friend Ron Mahovsky, who had customized his Python, had survived the Night of The War. Rourke, retrospectively, decided he should have asked Mahovsky to Metalife the CAR-15's magazines for added durability.

It was too late now—but many things were too late.

The microfilm projectors—why so many?

And he thought of Sarah, and Michael, and Annie. The children would have changed—not the time, but the experience. And Sarah—he closed his eyes.

Before the Night of The War, they had always argued over his "preoccupation," as she had called it, "with gloom and doom, preparing for the unthinkable"—his concerns with survival. She had seen guns as nothing more than weapons of destruction.

Rourke studied the profiled CAR-15 across his thighs.

It was hard to consider a rifle a weapon of destruction, considering the weapons unleashed on the Night of The War.

He closed his eyes—he remembered the flight across the United States that night—he could not forget it.

The children dying of burns in Albuquerque.

The teens who had called themselves the Guardians—in Texas. Their faces and their bodies scarred with radiation burns, their lives ending, their minds scarred and gone with the horror.

He opened his eyes, staring at the gun—he had saved lives with it, tried righting wrongs.

John Rourke closed his eyes again—he wondered if Sarah had changed—at all.

Chapter Seven

She looked at Annie — it was like Annie was trying to be her little carbon copy. One of the men in the Resistance — a black man, Tom — had given Annie a bandanna handkerchief, blue and white. And Annie wore it tied over her hair now, like Sarah herself had habitually worn one since The Night of The War. She thought about that — when she had cleaned house, or been baking bread she'd always — but there was no house to clean, no house at all.

Sarah Rourke licked her lips, getting up from the fire-blackened ridge pole of the destroyed barn — fallen now. She had found it a favorite place to sit when she'd been outside the underground survival bunker beneath the burned-out Cunningham farmhouse.

She started walking toward Annie, Annie pretending to read a book to one of the less seriously wounded Resistance men. Sarah had brought the man from the bunker for the fresh air. The generator that powered the ventilation system in the below-ground-level shelter needed fuel or foot-pedal power. Fuel was in short supply, and so were feet with nothing to do but ride a bicycle. The job was frequently falling to Michael. He had been an intrepid bike rider before The Night of The War and she thought that now Michael almost seemed to enjoy working the foot-powered generator. But foot power was not enough to pump sufficient air that the air smelled anything but stale and dirty. And so spent as much time outside as she could.

The wounded man's airing was just an excuse.

She wondered, suddenly, as she walked, what it would be like inside her husband's Retreat — if he found her. "When," she said under her breath, correcting herself.

She stopped walking, about midway between the burned shell of the barn and the gleaming whiteness of the corral fence where the quarter horses old Mr. Cunningham had raised once roamed. They were gone now — but so were Tildie and Sam, her horse and John's horse, the horses she had used with the children, the horses that had moved them out of danger, been like part of her family —

She stood there, wiping her hands along her blue-jeaned thighs — then resting her hands on her hips. Under her right hand she felt the butt of the Trapper .45 Bill Mulliner had given her. He should have met his Resistance contact by now, perhaps already be on his way back to report to Pete Critchfield.

Mary Mulliner — Bill's mother — it was written in the lines etched in her face, a fear for him, that she'd lose red-haired, blue-eyed Bill just like she had lost her husband — fighting in the Resistance against Russians and Brigands. The .45 had been Bill's father's gun — and now it was Sarah's.

She had already used it to save her life.

She rarely thought of it — it was so much a part of her now, carrying a gun, like wearing the blue and white bandanna with which she habitually covered her hair.

Little Annie was still pretending to read to the wounded Resistance fighter. Birds whistled in the trees.

Sarah closed her eyes — very tired. Would there be time to teach Annie Rourke to read — ever — and not just pretend?

Chapter Eight

General Ishmael Varakov sat on a park bench, halfway across the spit of land extending out into the lake toward the astronomy museum. The wind was stiff and cold off the lake there.

Beside him, Catherine sat. His secretary, the girl who wore her uniform skirts too long—a shy girl. A shy girl who had told him that she loved him when he had attempted to send her back to spend the last few days with her mother and her brother in the home he would never again visit beside the Black Sea. She had refused to go—he had let her stay.

He looked down at his left hand now—for some reason he yet didn't understand, his left hand clutched her right hand. She was young enough to be his daughter—or perhaps granddaughter.

She would not call him anything besides "comrade general"—and she whispered those words now.

"Yes, child," he nodded.

"We will all die?"

"Yes, child—all of us. A week, perhaps—if

that—" And thunder rumbled from the sky, a flash of chain lightning snaking low through gray clouds over the white-capped waters of Lake Michigan. But the lightning subsided, passed. "Very soon," he whispered to her, "very soon, Catherine—the lightning will not go away."

"I will miss it—if you can miss it, comrade general—being alive, I think."

He looked at her face—the rims of her eyes were moist. "You cry, child?"

She nodded yes.

"That you die, child? We will all die."

She shook her head no.

"Then why is it that you cry, child?"

"That I had to be told I would die—comrade general—before—before I—" and she looked away from him, Varakov feeling her hand in his, her nails digging into his flesh. It was life—sensation was life now, and he did not tell her to stop.

Chapter Nine

Rourke stopped the Harley-Davidson Low Rider, dismounting as he let down the stand.

Below him, in a shallow depression too small to be actually called a valley, was a burned farmhouse — or so it appeared to be. A barn too, also burned. There was a white fence, a corral fence, freshly painted it seemed, gleaming white against the blackness of the burned timbers of the two buildings. There was movement near the shell of the house.

Rourke removed his binoculars from the case, the lens caps already off, in the case bottom.

His hands were trembling.

It was near Mt. Eagle, it had apparently once been a horse farm. A sign, fallen down and broken in half, partially obscured by underbrush, had been at the end of the dried-mud-rutted ranch road, where the ranch road had met the blacktop.

The sign had read: Cunningham's Folly — Friends Welcome, Others Planted.

Apparently, it hadn't been planting season.

Both buildings, having been burned so completely, bore the marks of other than natural causes — Brigands.

Rourke raised the binoculars to his eyes, focusing them.

"Freeze!"

Rourke froze — whoever was behind him, whoever had spoken, was very good — very good.

Rourke held the binoculars at eye level, shifting his right hand slightly so the fingers of his left hand could reach under the storm sleeve of his bomber jacket. With all the Soviet activity, Rourke had hidden the little Freedom Arms .22 Magnum boot pistol he'd taken off the dead body of a Brigand, hidden it on a heavy rubber band butt downward on the inside of his right wrist. The four-round cylinder was one-round shy, the half-cocked hammer resting over an empty chamber.

"You must be an Indian to sneak up on me like that," Rourke said, not turning around, palming the little Freedom Arms gun under his left hand, still peering through the binoculars. There was a woman moving about the yard near the white corral fence.

"I been called 'nigger' lots, but ain't never been called no Indian, fella."

"There's a woman — young woman — down there by the corral fence — what's her name?"

He heard movement behind him.

"I asked her name."

He felt the muzzle of a gun at the back of his neck.

Rourke stepped back against it on his right foot, simultaneously snapping his left foot up and back, hearing a guttural sigh, feeling his heel connect with tissue and bone, his left arm moving as he half dodged, half fell right, sweeping up and against the muzzle of the gun — it was a Ruger Mini-14 stainless — knocking the rifle barrel hard left as the man holding it sagged forward, knees buckling.

Rourke half rolled, half wheeled, balanced on his right hand and left foot, his right leg snaking up and out, the toe of his combat boot impacting against the black rifleman's abdomen just above the belt.

Then Rourke was up, the little Freedom Arms boot pistol's hammer at full stand, the muzzle of the pistol against the black man's right ear as the man sagged to the ground.

"Don't move — you alone?"

"Fuck you — "

Rourke increased the pressure of the pistol against the man's ear. "It'd be awful dumb for you to make me shoot you — I think we're on the same side. Now — the name of the woman down by the corral fence — "

"Why the hell you wanna know — "

"Maybe she's my wife — "

"You the guy's who's the doctor — "

Rourke eased the three-inch barreled pistol away from the man's ear. He stood up, blocking the hammer with his thumb, his hands shaking too much to trust to lowering it at that instant.

"Her name is—"

The black man looked up—there was anger in his eyes, but surprise too—"Sarah Rourke—"

Rourke did something he rarely did.

His hands stopped shaking. He lowered the hammer on the little .22 Magnum and shifted it to his left hand.

With his right hand, John Thomas Rourke made the sign of the Cross.

Chapter Ten

The black Resistance fighter's name was Tom—
he said Annie was "the cutest little girl he'd ever
seen," and that Michael was more man than boy,
pulling his weight, and that Sarah was a tough
fighter, an angel of mercy—what held them together since the loss of David Balfry.

Rourke had said nothing about the Mulliner
boy.

And he walked now, his Harley left behind him
with the man named Tom—he had told the man he
was the quietest man he had never heard. But
Rourke put being surprised down more to himself
than to Tom's skills—his mind had been else-
where, his reactions turned off. Had Tom been a
Brigand, or a Russian—he would have been dead.

He walked on.

He could see Sarah's figure growing in defini-
tion as he bridged the gap of distance between the
depression's overlook and the farmyard near the
white corral fence.

Her dark brown hair was all but obscured by

what looked like a bandanna handkerchief. She wore a light blue shirt of some kind — it looked like a T-shirt. She looked, from the distance at least, like she looked when she worked in her studio, or about the house.

He walked on.

A small child, near a man propped beside a tree — too small, the child was, to be Michael. It was Annie.

She looked like a miniature of her mother.

Where was Michael?

He walked on, a thin, dark tobacco cigar in the left corner of his mouth, clenched tight between his teeth.

He lit it with cupped hands around his Zippo against the cool wind blowing up from the direction of the burned-out farm.

The CAR-15 was across his back, slung diagonally cross-body from his left shoulder.

The musette bag on his right side whacked out and back against his body as he took long strides, even strides in his combat-booted feet. The binocular case swayed and thumped at his right side, against the Pachmayr gripped butt of his Python there in the flap holster.

In the small of his back, where he'd placed it when he'd seen the Russians, was the two-inch barreled Colt Lawman .357 — the one he'd used to shoot the Brigand leader in that first confrontation after the massacre of the passengers from the airliner he had landed — less than perfectly — in the desert outside Albuquerque.

The black chrome Sting IA knife was tucked inside the waistband of his Levis on his left side.

He was barely conscious of the weight of the twin stainless Detonics pistols under his armpits beneath the battered brown leather bomber jacket.

He walked on.

The musette bag was heavy—he felt its weight. Spare magazines for the CAR-15.

On his gunbelt, he carried the holstered Python. Hanging from his trouser belt, was the Sparks Six-Pack with loaded Detonics magazines, the Six-Pack a gift from the submarine commander, Gunderson.

He inhaled the smoke into his lungs—memories.

Natalia's face. Paul's face—memories he could feel now.

The future was about to turn around, to notice him—he could feel it as it started at the growingly clear image of his wife, Sarah Rourke.

He walked on.

Chapter Eleven

"Momma?"

Half the women and a small percentage of the men in the world would react to the name, Sarah Rourke thought, turning around, seeing her son coming up from the bunker.

"Momma?"

"What is it, Michael?" and she felt herself smile.

But she saw past him, past his tall, straight little body, beyond the tousled brown hair that never stayed combed, beyond the brown eyes sometimes sparkling with curiosity, sometimes dull with weariness.

She saw a figure of a man, a man, tall, straight, dark hair like her son's hair, the wind catching it. There was an assault rifle slung from his body under his right arm—she could barely detect the shape of the barrel—it was across his back.

"Your father always carried a rifle like that—it never looked comfortable to—"

She stopped, staring.

She said it again. "Your father—your—Michael—" She was barely whispering.

46

He looked at her, then to where Annie was still pretending to read to the injured Resistance fighter, and then he looked behind him, beyond the gutted frame of the farmhouse.

"Daddy—"

Michael started to run.

Sarah looked—like a reaction—to Annie. Annie had dropped the book, was pulling the bandanna from her hair, her honey-colored hair caught in the wind as she ran. "Daddy!"

Sarah Rourke closed her eyes. "Please, Jesus— let it work—please," she whispered.

Sarah Rourke ran, toward the tall, dark-haired man in the leather jacket, shouting across the field, "John!"

Chapter Twelve

John Rourke started to run, toward the woman outdistancing the two children—toward Sarah, Michael, Annie. Sarah wasn't wearing a bra—he could tell that, because as she ran her fists were balled up and tucked up under her chest—she always ran like that if she just wore a shirt or blouse and no bra. Michael—he was taller, bigger-looking than he had been—fine-looking. Annie—her hair was longer, her smile something he had never forgotten.

As he ran, he stripped the CAR-15 from his shoulder, holding the rifle now by the pistol grip, almost like a balance pole for an acrobat.

He could hear her—"John!"

Rourke shouted the word: "Sarah!"

He threw himself into the run, hearing the children screaming to him, his eyes riveting to Sarah's face—one hundred yards now, ninety yards—"Sarah—" eighty yards, the tall grass in the field parting like an ocean wave in front of his feet, his mouth open gulping air, his hands out at his sides, the rifle weightless to him in his clenched right fist.

Twenty-five yards—he ran, Sarah's face clear to him, her right hand reaching up and tugging away the bandanna covering her head, her hair falling into the wind longer than he had seen it for years—ten yards. Five—

John Rourke swept his wife into his arms, their mouths finding each other, Rourke crushing her against him, feeling her body mold to his.

He buried his face in her neck for a moment, kissing her, inhaling her—

He kissed her hair as she pressed her head against his chest.

He looked down—Michael and Annie—"Daddy!" It was Annie, the smile.

John Rourke dropped to his knees, losing the CAR-15 in the high grass, folding his son and his daughter into his body—Sarah fell to her knees, her arms about his neck, holding him tight as he held the children.

"Daddy—" It was Michael—

John Rourke cried.

Chapter Thirteen

She was exhausted, but she was careful — not to show it. Because Paul Rubenstein seemed even more exhausted and the seriousness of his wound sustained at the hands of the Wildmen was something that worried her. It would heal well, but there had been much blood loss — the Wildman's spear had impaled Rubenstein's arm, and it had been some time before medical treatment had been available.

She killed the red light switch and stepped in behind Paul, into the Retreat.

"No need to close the inside door," Paul told her, leaning heavily against the natural rock beside the interior entrance door, the lights on in the Great Room now, his hand beside the switch. "Welcome home," he told her, looking at her, smiling.

"Paul — why don't I change your bandages — and make you comfortable — there's nothing that heavy that I can't load it into the truck — "

"Bullshit — like John'd say — " and then his eyes

50

lit behind his wire-framed glasses, smiling — "But you can drive the pickup —"

She only nodded — men were insane. . . .

They had gotten the truck ready quickly — Natalia had, forcing Paul to rest on the couch in the Great Room of the Retreat, hoping against hope that he would fall asleep. She could disable his bike and hers so he couldn't follow her, and he would be forced to rest. But he hadn't fallen asleep — and they drove, together, away from the Retreat now, down the mountain — she thought of it as Rourke's mountain but supposed on some map of northeastern Georgia somewhere it had a different name. But that didn't matter — it was his mountain. He had bought the property, forged the Retreat with his own hands, stocked it — he had prepared.

She felt a smile cross her lips — he was always prepared — almost.

And she felt something else at the thought — her love for him.

And it was, like he had said, "home" — now, forever. Whatever happened with Sarah, whatever happened with the world — she would be with John Rourke, however he wanted her with him. It was still a long drive to the hidden F-111 prototype and the cache of arms and ammunition and supplies.

The road was best built for foot travel, horseback or motorcycles — even the four-wheel drive of the truck was hard pressed, she realized, driving down from the Retreat, the Retreat doors secured again with their weights and balances locking system, the interior secured with its combination systems.

The truck's lights were out and she drove by the intermittent moonlight.

Thunder rumbled, illuminating the high, scattered clouds, the clouds seeming to be a rich blue when lit by the lightning.

Beside her, Paul Rubenstein was asleep.

She yawned, rolling the window of the camouflage-painted Ford pickup truck all the way down, forcing her eyes to stay open, putting her head partly out the window so the cold night breeze would help keep her awake.

She thought of a line by the American poet Robert Frost — ". . . miles to go before I sleep." Her favorite poets were Russian poets — but his words and thoughts seemed good to her.

Chapter Fourteen

She couldn't take her eyes off the guns—he only wore the double shoulder holsters, the ones he had always worn. The leather of the harness seemed a little dirty, but from so long on the trail, searching for her—her eyes shifted up to his eyes, flickering in the dull burn of the bare bulb suspended from the ceiling over the small card table in the far corner of the underground shelter.

Michael slept, and so did Annie—getting them to sleep had been hard, with their father newly returned. But she had convinced them that the next day, going to their new home at their father's Retreat would be full of excitement and wonder—she had not been able to convince herself.

She was nervous—John had told her about the death of Bill Mulliner—and she had wept more than she had thought she could. All that was fine, decent—all that was good. It was being destroyed forever.

Mary Mulliner sat by the edge of the card table, between Sarah and John.

At each side of the table, one dominated by John, sat men of the Resistance, Pete Critchfield opposite John, his cigar more foul-smelling than the one her husband puffed. To Rourke's right sat Tom—he had told her a little about his first encounter with her husband. To John Rourke's left—to her left though she sat back from the table, was Curley, the radio operator.

She watched her husband's eyes. Watched his lips as he took the cigar from his teeth, turning his face toward her, his eyes flickering toward Mary Mulliner, between them.

"Mrs. Mulliner—before we talk here—well—"

"Bill is dead," Mary Mulliner said, her hands awkward-looking on her trousered thighs— Mary had never been anything of a modern woman, Sarah thought, trying to remember if ever before had she seen the older woman wear pants. She didn't think so. And the hands just rested cupped inside one another between her thighs now.

Sarah Rourke heard John Rourke clear his throat. "He died—well, very bravely. He was trying to save some other Resistance people who'd been shot up by Brigands—I don't think he was in a lot of pain—he—"

Mary Mulliner began to cry—to sob, heavy sobs. Sarah slid from the folding card table chair to the floor beside Mary's chair, on her knees, reaching up to fold her right arm about the older woman's shoulders. The woman's head rested against her right shoulder, Sarah hugging her to herself.

Her husband began again to talk. "The last things he said—well—he told me, Bill did—'Tell my mom I love her—and tell Mrs. Rourke good-bye.'"

Sarah looked into her husband's eyes—she cried, her throat tight, so tight she could barely breathe.

Chapter Fifteen

It had taken better than an hour for Sarah to calm Mary Mulliner, and to calm herself, her throat sore-feeling, her eyes burning, her sinuses strangely clear as she had returned to the Samsonite card table around which her husband, John Rourke, the de facto Resistance leader, Pete Critchfield, the black man, Tom, and Curley sat. The air was blue-gray under the glow of the bulb with the cigar smoke. At the far end of the underground shelter—like a huge concrete basement—she could hear the rhythm of the bicycle generator being pedaled.

She was happy it wasn't Michael.

"Sarah—glad you're back," Pete Critchfield nodded. "Pull up a chair." Her husband stood, pushing a chair for her as she sat. Tom started to stand—neither of the other two men moved. "I'm tryin' to convince your husband here to throw in with all of us in the Resistance against the Commies, rather than take you away from us."

John Rourke said nothing. Critchfield cleared his throat loudly, cigar smoke filtering from his nostril. "What about it, John?" Sarah asked him.

He looked at her—a stern look. "I'm getting you and the children to safety at the Retreat. The weather, the thunder and lightning—all of it. Something's happening and I need to find out what so we can prepare for it and survive it. After all that, if there's a chance, sure—I'll help the Resistance. My friend Paul will help—but you and Michael and Annie. I don't want you having any part of it."

"Yeah—I don't mean to interfere between a man and his wife, John, but—well, hell—" Critchfield started.

John Rourke turned his eyes away from her and stared across the table at Critchfield—Pete Critchfield fell silent.

Tom spoke. "What Pete means, man—your lady there. She's one of us. Fights better than a lot of us—especially me," and Tom laughed. "She's good with a gun and all, but so's your son, I hear. But more than that—she's well—hell—a strong lady, and smart. We lose her and well—even the boy, and little Annie—she keeps us goin'—but we lose Sarah here, man—I mean, I know she's your wife and belongs with you, but—we can't get somebody else—nobody—ain't nobody'll replace her to us, ya know?"

Sarah looked at Tom—his eyes coal-black, the whites slightly yellowed, were warm, deep against his dark chocolate skin—and he smiled at her. She felt her lips raise in a smile, then looked at her husband. He wasn't looking at her.

She couldn't see John's face other than in profile, saw the cigar, unlit, clamped tight in the left corner of his mouth. His lips were drawn back, his teeth so white she sometimes wondered if he were really human. He had shaved before the meeting, before the meager meal from their stores. His face looked chiseled in stone, like she imagined somehow God should look — or if not God, some god.

His voice was low, a whisper — barely audible so that you strained to listen to him, the result that his words were always heard, always understood — and the feeling behind his words.

"Sarah's my wife — I'm taking her with me. All of us are fighting what's happening — in our own ways. Raising Michael and Annie if we all live long enough for her to do that is the best way I know to fight the Communists, to try to make something out of America again — to rebuild. That's what she'll be doing. Period — end of discussion."

If it were possible, he seemed to clamp the cigar more tightly, his jaw set harder.

Sarah — her hands shaking — fought within her thousands, millions of years of what if meant to be a woman. Standing up, she whispered, "Damn you —" and she walked away from the table, starting for the outside.

She needed to breathe.

Chapter Sixteen

"Whatchya think that is, over yonder there, Bob?"

Bob raised the binoculars he'd stolen in a fight days after The Night of The War—binoculars stolen from a five and ten cent store they had been looting in Commerce, Georgia. The man with the rifle in the store—not a very big man—had been tough enough and good enough with a gun that twelve of Bob's friends—he thought of their names now—had died. Command had sort of devolved to him—Bob—and he had ordered a withdrawal. The little finger of his left hand was gone, shot off. A parting gift from the owner of the five and ten cent store.

He stared through the binoculars now. They weren't made for using at night, at least he didn't figure they were. He'd thrown away the box with the owner's manual. All he could see were dim shapes—what looked like some burned buildings and a white fence that almost seemed to glow.

He put down the binoculars, saying to the man beside him, "Dunno, Lyle—maybe jes' some folks hiding out from guys like us — don't think they's no Russians. Maybe some of them Resistance heroes — hell," and he spat into the grass in front of his engineer boots.

"I saw me a light for a second — like some door was bein' opened. Hey — lookee there," Lyle rasped.

Bob followed where Lyle pointed — with his eyes.

Near the white fence — someone was walking.

"They'll be a guard or two, betchya," Lyle said.

"If it is them Resistancers, we can get us some food, some more guns and stuff — shit — "

"We gonna take 'em, Bob?"

Bob looked at Lyle, then up the defile behind them. He had forty men — all of them with guns of one kind or another — and all of them pretty good with their bikes.

"Fuck, yeah — yeah," and Bob spat again between his boots.

Chapter Seventeen

She hadn't meant it—not wanting to damn him—she loved him. But always—he was always the one who was right. No other opinion mattered—never—nothing. "Damnit," she snarled, hitting her little fist into the fence crosspiece. The crosspiece rattled.

She heard movement beyond the barn—it would be Jack. It was his tour on guard— "Just me, Jack," she hissed loudly into the night.

After a moment, she heard him call back, "Right, Mrs. Rourke!"

She started walking along the fence.

Her hair was up—the first time she'd had it up since the attack on the Mulliner farm. She had taken the blue denim skirt from her pack, the only skirt she had—she wore it still, with a blue chambray shirt like the ones her husband habitually wore—this given her by one of the Resistance men. It was too big for her, the sleeves rolled up above her elbows, all but the top button buttoned and still showing more neckline than she liked, and it bloused like a balloon around her waist inside the waistband of her skirt.

She only had track shoes—she looked like a clown, she thought. Like an over-age urchin. And she had her belt around her waist with the holster for the Trapper .45—trying to dress up for her husband, she still hadn't been willing to abandon the gun.

The spare magazine for it was in the left side pocket of her skirt—she remembered that as she stabbed her hands into her pockets now, walking still beside the fence.

Why did he have to be like that?

He'd come after her—they'd argue, she'd give in. "Shit," she whispered.

She looked up—lightning illuminated the scattered clouds, the moon bright—almost bright enough to read by.

She kept walking.

Chapter Eighteen

John Rourke stood over his children, watching them sleep. Michael rolled over—opened his eyes. "Hi, Daddy."

Rourke dropped to his knees beside the children. It was a far corner of the bunker, a blanket hung to make a triangle with the corner walls. There was another air mattress beside the one on which the children lay—it was empty. Sarah slept there, he knew—she had shown him their quarters.

"Shh," he told his son. He raised his right first finger to his lips, his voice low. "Don't wanna wake your sister, Michael."

"Where's Mommy?"

"Outside—"

"What's the matter?"

"Nothing to worry about—I'm taking you and your sister and your mother home tomorrow—you'll have a ball. So much to do at the Retreat—books, music—I've got a videocassette recorder there—movies, educational programs—you can learn about astronomy, about the human body,

about science — physics and chemistry — all of it —
for you and Annie to learn from —"

"Can we play outside?"

Rourke sucked in his breath. "Sometimes — but
the idea of the Retreat is that it's kind of secret —
like a secret hiding place, ya know? But you can
play with Paul — you can call him Uncle Paul —
he's my best friend. And —"

"And Natalia?"

Rourke closed his eyes.

"Mommy told me she'd asked you about some
Russian lady and you said her name was Natalia
and she'd be <u>living</u> with us from now on."

Rourke nodded. "You can play with Natalia,
too — Annie'll like her a lot — so will you, son."

"But aren't the Russians the ones who started
everything — like The War, and all the trouble —"

"But Natalia didn't start it. She saved my life —
more than once. Natalia and Paul — the three of us
have been searching for you and your sister and
your mother. She's a good friend — you'll like her,
be happy with her."

"Is Natalia going to marry — what did you say
his name was —"

"Paul."

"Is Natalia going to marry Uncle Paul?"

Rourke closed his eyes again, then opened
them, seeing his son in the gray light. "No — she
isn't — no —"

"Well, why is she staying with us, Daddy?"

Rourke swallowed. "She's a good friend to Paul
and me. And in helping us look for you guys, well,
she kind of got in trouble with the KGB —"

"That's the Russian CIA, isn't it?"

"Yeah—sort of—but different in a lot of ways."

"Is Natalia a spy, like you were?"

"Sort of—but she's through with that now—just wants to be with us, be our friend, help things get right again—like that—it's a long story. Complicated—kind of."

"I'm not sleepy—you can tell me," Michael insisted.

"I'm sleepy," Rourke smiled in the darkness. "I'll tell you all about it later—all about it. I hear you've been taking good care of your mother and sister—give me your hand," and Rourke reached his right hand out in the darkness, found his son's vastly smaller, but solid, firm hand—he clasped it tight.

"Oww—"

Rourke laughed, low, soft. "You've turned into one hell of a good man, son. And I'll be needing your help a lot as we go along."

"Momma tell you that I—"

"That man at the farm—that you killed him. I'm sorry you had to do that—but I'm glad you were there to protect your mother and sister—yeah—she told me. And at the Mulliner place—looks like all those times we went out back and fooled with the guns came in handy, huh?" and he clasped his son's shoulders in the darkness. "But you can put all that behind you now—go back to growing up. You've done a lot of that, but there's a lot of growing to do and everything. I'm proud of you."

"I'm glad you came back—Mommy never

stopped talking about when you'd find us. Things would get kind of bad—we'd be cold, or there'd be Brigands or Russians all around us—but Momma always said you'd find us."

"You think this'll make her happy—the Retreat, I mean? What do you think?"

"Maybe—I'm not sure. But she wants to be with you."

"I love her—being a grown-up isn't all it's cracked up to be, kid," and Rourke bent over his son, finding the boy's face, kissing his forehead.

He heard automatic weapons fire from outside. "Stay here," and Rourke was up, running. Sarah was outside.

Chapter Nineteen

His revolver, his CAR-15—along with his other gear—were too far away. Only the twin stainless Detonics pistols, these in the double Alessi rig across his back, and the six spare magazines in the Sparks Six-Pack on his trouser belt, Rourke ran into the night, squinting his eyes tight shut against the velvet blackness punctuated by bursts of gunfire, counting to ten, opening his eyes, more accustomed now to the darkness after the dim light of the bunker through which he had run.

Both Detonics pistols came into his hands, his thumbs jacking back the hammers as his fists balled around them.

"Sarah! Sarah!"

Men on motorcycles filled the yard between the bunker beneath the burned-out farmhouse and the white-fenced corral, the house, the corral, and the shell of the burned barn making the points of a triangle. And the triangle seemed alive to him with movement, with gunfire, with shouts and curses and the revving of engines. Brigands—he lost count after he hit twelve, and there were at least three times that many, likely more, he gauged. Both pistols in his clenched fists discharged together, two men on motorcycles—they were Brigands all—racing toward him across the yard. Both men fell, their bikes spinning out, Rourke jumping clear of the one to his left, firing a third round, killing a man on foot rushing him, the man with an assault rifle.

"Sarah!" He screamed the word into the night, not seeing his wife, not hearing a scream.

His jaw set, the tendons in his neck something he could feel as they distended.

"Sarah!"

There was the boom of a .45 from his left and he wheeled toward it, firing a fourth round from his pistols at another of the Brigands. And then he saw her, a pistol visible in her hands in the glare of a motorcycle headlight, the biker bearing down on her, Rourke raising both pistols to shoot the man down, two bikers thrusting between him and the intended target.

Rourke fired both pistols again, nailing one biker only, then firing the pistol in his left hand twice more, killing the second man, the head almost splitting under the double impact, visible as the ground was suddenly bathed in moonlight.

There were two rounds apiece in each gun, no time to reload, Sarah's small pistol—about the size of his own Detonics guns, the gun he'd seen her wearing throughout the late afternoon and evening—flashing fire twice before he could shoot, the Brigand biker's body blown from the bike seat, the bike crashing into the glaring whiteness of the

68

fence, splintering the wood there with a thunderlike cracking sound.

He could see Sarah, stepping away, turning, punching the little .45 out in both hands. A man was rushing her from behind with an assault rifle.

Rourke's pistols fired, her pistol fired, the Brigand's body twisting once, then again and again.

Rourke broke into a run, firing out both pistols before he reached her, killing one more of the Brigands, wounding another as the man fell from his bike, clasping his left shoulder.

Both pistols empty, Rourke rammed the one from his left hand into his belt, dumping the magazine for the right-hand gun, ramming a fresh one up the butt, his right thumb working down the slide stop as his left hand pocketed the empty magazine, Sarah shouting to him. "John! Behind you!"

Rourke wheeled, dropping, punching the Detonics out in his right fist, the boom of a .45 behind him, the riot shotgun-armed Brigand stumbling, falling back as Rourke's pistol fired then, the second impact high as the man's body jackknifed, the neck exploding as the left side of it was blown away, blood spurting in a fine spray Rourke could see on the air.

He was up then, grabbing the riot shotgun from the dead man, upping the safety on the little Detonics, wheeling, working the riot shotgun's trigger, the stubby-barreled pump's twelve-gauge slug flaring in the moonlit darkness, the shot column disintegrating the face of a man rushing him.

Rourke tromboned the shotgun, beside Sarah

now, Sarah's .45 booming once, a Brigand shot off his bike.

He looked at her—the spent magazine was falling into her left hand, the spare magazine between her left thumb and forefinger, encircled by the digits, going up the butt of the pistol, then her hand twisting as the magazine was thumped into a locked position, her right thumb working down the slide stop.

Rourke raised the riot shotgun, firing once, then again and again, three Brigand bikers going down, Sarah beside him shouting, "The bike!"

He jumped clear, the machine from the second man impacting against the fence, bursting through it.

Her .45 fired once, then again and again, two bikers down.

Men were pouring from the bunker now, assault rifles and riot shotguns firing, the Brigand attackers falling back.

Rourke tromboned the pump—the shotgun was empty. He threw it down, grabbing for the partially loaded Detonics.

He started forward, shouting to Sarah, "Stay here!"

"No!"

He looked at her, then started forward anyway, his wife beside him, their .45s like pulsing torches in the darkness, Brigand bikers falling as gunfire rained around them.

He heard Annie scream—it was her voice.

Rourke wheeled, reloading the Detonics as he moved, running now toward the bunker.

A Brigand with an assault rifle, a bayonet fixed at the muzzle, Annie bare-legged in a long white T-shirt, hitting at the man with something.

Rourke raised the Detonics to fire, heard Sarah screaming, "Annie!"

Rourke had the Brigand's head under the muzzle of the Detonics. A tight shot, he started the squeeze.

There was a burst of assault rifle fire, somehow muffled-sounding, the Brigand's body crumpling, sagging, falling forward, the assault rifle discharging into the ground, Annie screaming again.

Rourke stopped.

Michael stood in the light of the bunker doorway, an M-16 in his hands, the dead Brigand at his feet.

Rourke wheeled, fired out the Detonics pistol into two men coming up on the right, buttoning out the magazines from both pistols to the ground, reloading as he sidestepped toward his son and daughter, Sarah firing beside him.

"I'm empty," she shouted.

Rourke handed her one of the twin Detonics pistols—their eyes met for an instant in the moonlight bathing the triangular piece of ground that made the farmyard.

"I was wrong—" He said it once, simply, as she took the pistol from him.

"So was I—"

There was a shouted curse, a rattle of assault rifle fire and the roar of motorcycle engines, Rourke half dropping into a crouch, Sarah to his right, both firing simultaneously as four Brigand

71

bikers roared down on them—one man down, then another, then a third, both hands flying to his chest as the bike went out of control, then the fourth man, screaming as he skidded on his bike into the wreck of the barn, the motorcycle's gas tank somehow igniting—an explosion, orange-tipped yellow flames with a black and yellow fireball belching upward into the night air at the center.

Rourke reached down to one of the dead men—the one Michael had killed. A strap from his binoculars was tangled in the assault rifle—Rourke ripped it away. As he pried the left hand from the front handguard of the M-16, he noticed the little finger was missing—it looked like it had been shot away.

He picked Annie up into this arms—she held a policeman's nightstick in her right hand and it fell to the ground as he crushed her against him.

He looked at his son. "Thank you—"

Chapter Twenty

It was like solving a puzzle, Nehemiah Rozhdestvenskiy told himself.

"Damn this," he murmured, blinking his eyes as he looked up from the litter of papers. "A man could go blind—" he began, not finishing it.

He stood up, lighting a cigarette.

Tired.

A puzzle. Intelligence reports from before The Night of The War, comparing these with areas that had survived the bombing, the missile strikes.

The Eden Project. If the astronaut had not been killed—died of his heart attack so shortly after the duel between the American Rourke and his predecessor, Vladmir Karamatsov.

The astronaut might have known.

Rozhdestvenskiy inhaled on his cigarette, the intake of breath making a light whistling sound.

He returned to his desk under the fluorescent tube fixture, studying the sheaves of reports, data—

The Eden Project had launched from the Kennedy Space Center in Florida—just before the hits on the center had destroyed it. What had remained had been searched, but further searching was impossible after the complete destruction of peninsular Florida in the massive quakes in the wake of the slippage of the artificial faultline created by the bombing.

He made himself assume that the answer was not beneath the ocean.

California — but the bombing on The Night of The War had triggered the San Andreas faultline — and there was no California.

The triangle —

He walked to the wall to his left, beside his desk.

He found Bevington, Kentucky's approximate location — the site of the factory that had been utilized in the manufacture of materials critical to The Eden Project. But the factory had been destroyed before he could find what he had sought.

"Triangle," he said in English.

In his mind he formed one leg of a triangle between Bevington, Kentucky and the crosshatched area where peninsular Florida had once been, to Cape Canaveral and the Kennedy Space Center.

He looked to the west across the map.

There was only one other place — and somehow Karamatsov must have known of it, the reason why a KGB base had been established at the overrun Air Force Base in Texas.

He drew the other leg of the triangle, Bevington, Kentucky and the factory there representing the triangle's apex.

His eye drew the baseline — between the Kennedy Space Center and Houston, Texas.

"The Johnson Space Center," he whispered.

After the Texas volunteer militia and U.S. II forces had retaken the base, Karamatsov and Major Tiemerovna barely escaping with their lives, Soviet freedom of action in Texas had been severely reduced.

"The Johnson Space Center—"

He turned to the telephone on his desk—waiting an instant. If he were wrong, there was really no other place to look and he would be dead. They would all be dead.

He lifted the receiver. "This is Colonel Rozhdestvenskiy—the Elite Corps strike force duty officer—I wish to speak with him immediately—"

The cigarette had burned down between his fingers and yellowed his flesh.

Chapter Twenty-one

She leaned against the fuselage of the plane, the prototype F-111. One more crate remained, M-16 rifles. She looked skyward—the horizon was pink-tinged, thunder rumbling in the east, streaks of lightning across the pink line between day and night.

She could hear Paul coming back from the camouflaged Ford pickup—and she turned to watch him. He moved like a man twice his age, his left arm stiff at his side.

Natalia turned quickly away from him, to the crate of rifles, reaching out for it, drawing it toward her—it was only twenty feet or so to the truck and perhaps—

"Hey—what the hell are you doin'?"

"I'm trying to move the crate—what's it look like, Paul?"

She felt him shove past her, felt, heard the pain it caused his arm as they made contact. His right hand was beside hers on the crate's rope handle, wrenching the crate away from her at an awkward angle.

"I take one end, you take the other — just like we've been doing," he said, not looking at her.

"I can do it — your arm —"

"Bullshit — your abdomen, probably still weak from the surgery — all I need is for you to rupture that area where John operated — now get out —"

Her left hand went against his chest as she turned to face him, shoving him back. "All I need is for you to die — get your arm bleeding again. Bullshit to you, too, Paul!"

She was screaming at him.

She stopped.

Rubenstein leaned forward, against the fuselage. He was laughing.

Natalia, too, felt herself begin to laugh. "What do you say we just leave this crate of rifles, huh?" he smiled.

"What do you say we just carry it like the other ones — hmm? That's a better idea."

"Yeah — it is a good idea — and you're a good lady," and then he turned to face her fully, and as his right arm moved out to her, she leaned her head against his chest.

Without his strength — not the physical kind, despite her sex she was his equal in physical stamina and endurance, though he was better in agility — life would have been sadder for her.

Chapter Twenty-two

Mary Mulliner stood beside the entrance to the bunker, the children pressed against her as she hugged them, John Rourke stood next to Sarah Rourke, beside the dented light blue pickup truck Pete Critchfield had scrounged for them—like Rourke's own pickup, which he imagined by now Natalia and Paul had used to empty the F-111 and ferry the supplies to the Retreat, this too was a Ford.

It was a "loan," but both Rourke and Critchfield had known the likelihood of the truck's being returned was remote to the point of nonexistence.

Rourke held his wife's right hand in his left, his right hand holding the scoped CAR-15. The golden retriever belonging to Mary Mulliner ran between Sarah and where Mary and the children stood—it yelped.

It looked like a good dog, Rourke thought.

He let go of his wife's hand, to glance at the black-faced Rolex Submariner he wore. It was nearly eight-thirty.

The Harley was packed, ready.

"I know,'" Sarah told him softly. "But she loves them—always acted like a grandmother to them, or an aunt. I can't just say—"

But then Mary Mulliner's voice, from across the yard, cut her off. "John Rourke—I don't know if you know what you got here. These two children—and this boy of yours is more of a man than most men I've ever heard tell of. And your wife—she's been pinin' for you, John Rourke. Keep her good."

"Yes, ma'am—I intend to," Rourke nodded.

Then Mary Mulliner started across the yard. Michael and Annie hugged against her hips as she walked.

The dog was barking maddeningly.

"Hush," she hissed to the dog, and the golden obeyed, stretching out at her feet as she stopped a yard away from Rourke and his wife. "The dog—misses Bill, I guess," and she started to smile, then burst into tears. Sarah folded the older woman in her arms and hugged her tightly.

Rourke watched, felt his children tugging at him. Affection, he suddenly realized, had always been hard for him.

He closed his eyes as the golden retriever started barking again.

Chapter Twenty-three

She drove the truck, tears in her eyes, Annie sitting — quietly — beside her.

Ahead of her was John Rourke, riding behind him on the Harley-Davidson sat Michael, Michael's hair blowing in the wind, as was her husband's — Michael was his miniature — in almost all ways.

In the side-view West Coast mirror — cracked by a bullet — she could see them standing there, Pete Critchfield, Tom, Mary Mulliner — the others.

Sarah Rourke looked down at her T-shirt — she had changed back into her normal clothes after the gunfight, no time for sleep, for rest — only time to prepare for the trek to the Retreat.

Pinned to the front of her T-shirt — she felt at once stupid and proud — was a Silver Star. The medal had been given Pete Critchfield's son who had died years earlier in the Viet Nam War.

Pete, pinning it to her T-shirt, startling her as he'd reached for her, had said, "Sarah — this war, well — we don't have no medals, nothin' for bravery. Like you've been ever since we met you. You hadn't killed those first coupla Brigand bikers last night, no tellin' if'n they'd have got down into the bunker and maybe killed us all—or a lot of us, leastwise. So—my boy won it, then got blown up by one of them mortar attacks—near the DMZ. So—it's your medal now—earned it just as much as he did, I reckon," and he had kissed her.

She looked down at the medal again.

She didn't need the Silver Star to remember Pete Critchfield, or Mary Mulliner's husband's pistol to remember young Bill who had given it to her.

She would remember David Balfry. The black man, Tom. Curley, the radio specialist. Mary Mulliner—remember them all, her family for a while.

Until her dying day.

She upshifted as she finished the turn out of the burned-down quarter horse farm.

The Cunningham place.

Chapter Twenty-four

The camouflaged Ford was parked, the cases of rifles and ammunition and medical gear and other supplies from the aircraft in the truck bed — Natalia too exhausted to bother moving them, Paul too weak.

She had insisted he go to bed — he had insisted on a shower. She had been too tired to argue it with him.

She sat, now, on the floor just outside the bathroom, listening for the sounds of him in the shower, afraid he was too weak to keep standing. She had offered to bathe him — and he had actually blushed. She smiled at the thought.

Love was a strange thing.

Her love for Paul was deep friendship, her love for Rourke something else entirely.

But Natalia wasn't certain what.

There was a loud squeaking noise and she heard a gasped "Shit!"

She was on her feet, inside the bathroom, ripping open the shower.

She dropped to her knees beside the tub, bending into it, Rubenstein's left arm dripping blood, Rubenstein collapsed in the back of the shower, the blood washing across his naked body, making a tiny stream of pinkish red toward the drain, his right leg drawn up, his left outstretched.

Natalia was up, stepping into the bathtub, careful of her footing, her left hand turning down the shower, her right hand reaching out for Paul.

His head raised, his eyes odd-seeming without his glasses on — she sometimes forgot they ever came off. His speech slurred a little, he whispered, "Slipped, I guess — ha," and he forced a smile.

"Did you hit your head?" she said leaning over him. As her eyes glanced down, she saw him coming erect between his legs.

"Get out of here —"

"I'm going to see if you're all right —"

"I haven't been this close to —"

"I know," she smiled. "There's nothing to be embarrassed about — it's a normal reaction — you haven't got any clothes on, that's all —"

And Rubenstein laughed, "This is stupid."

"What's stupid?" she said, feeling the back of his head, parting his wet hair to see if he'd injured himself.

"I'm naked in the shower with the most beautiful woman I've ever seen and what am I doing — wishing for an erection to go down because I'm embarrassed."

She kissed his forehead quickly, stepping out of the shower, reaching out to help him to his feet.

"That didn't help me," he smiled. . . .

She had stopped the bleeding, bandaging his

arm after forcing him to let her finish washing him — men were babies, she thought. As if any woman could reach maturity and not know what a penis looked like.

And she put him to bed, giving him some of the painkiller John had prescribed for him, covering him, turning off the light, and going immediately back into the bathroom. It needed cleaning after the flood from the shower. She started working at that, getting up her bootprints, drying the floor.

She badly wanted a shower, but more badly wanted a cigarette, leaving the bathroom, walking down the three steps and into and across the Great Room to the couch. Her guns, still holstered, were on the coffee table. She found her cigarettes in the black canvas bag that doubled as purse and light-load backpack. She lit one, inhaling the smoke deep into her lungs, sitting back in the couch.

She stared up at the ceiling for a while — the stalactites there reminding her of something she didn't wish to be reminded of, really, but making her laugh. "Paul," she smiled.

She rolled onto her belly, supporting herself on her elbows.

On the end table beside the couch she saw the photograph — Rourke, Sarah, Michael, and Annie. Michael was his father — the perfect miniature, she thought. And someday, if they all survived that long, he would be the perfect duplicate rather than perfect miniature.

She looked at Sarah's face. "What kind of woman are you, Sarah?"

She rolled onto her back then, closing her eyes,

still smoking her cigarette. She was past falling asleep. If Rourke found his family, or if he found that they could not be found, it would forever change her life.

She could not sleep.

She thought about Sarah Rourke—how was it to be the wife of John Rourke? To cook for him, to keep his clothes clean? How was it to sleep with him?

She—Natalia—had slept beside him, in his arms. He had kissed her. But because of Sarah, he would not—

Natalia sat up, stubbing out her cigarette.

She decided to light another one.

Alone in the Great Room, through an exhaled cloud of gray smoke, she told herself, "I would be blindingly lucky at cards."

Chapter Twenty-five

Rourke skidded the Harley to an arcing stop—"Shit," he snarled. Coming around the bend of the two-lane highway they rode, Michael behind him on the Low Rider, Sarah driving the borrowed pickup truck, Annie with her, there was a Soviet motorized patrol.

The lead men on motorcycles slowed their bikes, stopped them, raising AKs, one of them shouting in poor English, "To halt—to halt! To raise the hands!"

Rourke raised his right hand, snatching at the Python in the hip holster, rasping to Michael, "Hang on tight, son!" He double-actioned the Metalifed six-inch .357 twice, the Mag-Na-Ported Colt rock steady in his balled right fist, the Russian who'd spoken, then taken both slugs, falling backward across his motorcycle, rolling to the roadway surface.

The second Russian biker was sweeping the muzzle of his AKM to fire—Rourke emptied the remaining four shots from the Python's cylinder into the man's center of mass, the AKM starting to fire, into the road surface, then up, Rourke passing the revolver back to Michael—"Here—hold this—barrel's hot—" The Harley, Rourke wrenched it around, gunning the engine, shouting to the truck, "Sarah—get out of here!"

But the vehicle was already backing up, cutting a ragged, bumping, lurching arc in reverse, the light blue Ford pickup shuddering visibly, the engine roaring, a screech of tires as the pickup cut a sharp left down the highway, Rourke almost up even to it.

Sarah was shouting something as he came level with the cab—Rourke couldn't hear over the engine noises, the slipstream, and the gunfire coming from behind them.

But he knew what she wanted—he nodded to her, raising his left hand, then slashing it down quickly. The Ford started into a skidding stop, Rourke slowing the Harley, stopping beside the truck cab. Sarah was leaning across the seat, the passenger side door opening fast, bouncing back on its hinges.

"Michael—into the truck—gimme my gun—you and your sister—down on the floor!"

He half threw the boy from behind him on the bike saddle to Sarah's hands reaching across Annie, crushing her, it seemed, against the seatback—but Annie was reaching for him, too—"Got him," Sarah shouted, Rourke slamming the door as his son cleared it, gunning the Harley as he holstered the empty Python, the Ford peeling out, gravel bits and a cloud of dust in its wake.

The CAR-15 — Rourke swung it forward on its sling, earing back the bolt, both hands on it tensioned against the sling, the stock collapsed. He started pumping the trigger — Russian soldiers, some running on foot, Russian bikers behind them — he fired into the lead elements, AK fire pouring back toward him.

He fired out the magazine, changing sticks, working the bolt release, then cutting the bike into a tight left and gunning the machine out — assault rifle fire tore into the road's surface on both sides of him — he could hear ricocheting sounds as bullets hammered into the rocks on the right side of the road — or perhaps his machine.

He ripped one of the twin stainless Detonics pistols from the leather under his left armpit, reaching around behind him, jacking the hammer back, firing once, twice, a third time — it was useless.

Upping the safety, he rammed the cocked and locked pistol into his belt, lowering his body over the Harley, gunning the engine — faster.

The pickup was dead ahead — he was gaining on it — gunfire rained around him, the roaring of Soviet bikes making his ears ring.

His wife — his son — his daughter — "Damn!" He shouted the word — maybe heaven would hear him, he thought.

The wind of the slipstream tore at him, stinging at his ears, his forehead, Rourke feeling his lips drawing back from his teeth — he didn't want to see his face.

The road angled sharply upward and into a curve, Sarah taking it fast, he saw — too fast? The Ford's rear end seemed to fishtail, the truck lurching, rising up and down on its shocks, then vanished around the curve. Rourke took the curve in a wide arc, cutting into the oncoming lane, skidding off the far lane and into the loose dirt and gravel of the shoulder, his feet out, balancing him, dragging as he fought to control the machine. His hands worked — the machine was pulling ahead — Rourke gunned the engine, gravel spraying up around him, pelting at his exposed hands, making pinging sounds against the steel of the Harley —

The exhaust — he could hear it thunder under him, behind him.

Back on the road — low over the Harley, gunfire tearing into the pines beyond the road shoulder, ripping into the tarmac under him, gravel and bullet fragments spraying around him, sparks on the roadside as bullets impacted small stones.

His lips drawn back tight, his neck — the tendons something he could feel distending — He let out the Harley — to catch the truck.

He was out of the curve, still climbing, the blue Ford pickup about a city block's length ahead as he leaned into his machine.

More gunfire, a stillness for an instant as the Soviet column must have taken the curve.

Rourke had the half-shot-out Detonics back

in his right fist, thumbing down the safety, swinging left in the Harley's saddle, keeping low over the machine, firing once, twice, a third time—the lead Soviet biker's machine skidding from under him, spilling the man onto the highway, the biker nearest behind him, jumping his machine to clear his comrade, the machine out of control, the man and the machine separating in midair. The bike crashed down—a Soviet truck behind the bikers skidding, losing control—in an instant shooting across the oncoming lanes and over the shoulder, impacting against a stand of pines.

Rourke leaned into his machine again, ramming the spent pistol into his hip pocket—riding.

He glanced back again—he had stalled the column.

Ahead, Sarah's truck was slowing. "Why?" He shrieked the word into the wind of the slipstream.

Michael—he could see the boy—Sarah's M-16—he was firing it through the open passenger window—ahead of them.

The truck was doing a high-speed reverse, Michael's head and the rifle tucked back inside, the pickup lurching onto the shoulder on Rourke's side, the near shoulder, gravel and dirt spraying up as the truck's rear wheels fought for traction, then the pickup bisecting the highway, crossing the oncoming lane, bouncing up and over the far shoulder, then disappearing below the rim of the highway.

"Why!"

Rourke looked behind him—the Russians were coming again, bikers riding low-profiled against their machines, men in open-topped transport trucks firing assault rifles.

Where the Ford pickup had been, ahead now Rourke could see what had made Sarah turn, leave the road—Brigands.

Men and women in pickup trucks, men on motorcycles, some with women riding behind them—assault rifles, shotguns—all bristled from the backs of the trucks.

Rourke arced the Harley right, then cutting a sharp left as he slowed, skidding, losing the bike, the bike going out from under him, Rourke's left leg out, his left foot all that kept the machine from crashing down, from skidding away, his arms aching as he wrestled the machine almost upright—he gunned the engine, shifting his weight right, the machine righting itself, then Rourke lowering his body over it as he cut across the road, gunfire from both sides of him now— Brigands shooting at him and at the Russians, Russians shooting at him and at the Brigands—

The road shoulder, Rourke trying to slow the bike—the edge of the ground beyond the shoulder, gravel and dust kicking up around him, gunfire from both sides—

The ground dropped into a steep slope, pine tree stumps speckling it, rocks and boulders and high grass, too. He jumped the Harley over a hummock, the machine coming down hard, Rourke fighting to control it. The Ford was ahead, slowly moving, rocking and bouncing —

Rourke balanced out the machine, slowing his speed, his combat-booted feet dragging both sides as he took the grade.

He looked back once — Brigands by the edge of the road — Russians, too — gunfire loud behind him.

But they were firing at each other.

Chapter Twenty-six

There were men moving along the ground beneath him — some of them, as he watched the sandy ground, raised rifles, firing — but the helicopter was at too high an altitude for gunfire from conventional weapons to reach him. It was like an American Western movie, but one where the director had lost all sense of the classic unities. There were pickup trucks riding alongside men on horseback — and there were cowboy hats everywhere.

There had been rumors that the leadership of the Texas volunteer militia had changed drastically after the death of their man Randan Soames — and intelligence reports Rozhdestvensky had been receiving confirmed that. And now his own eyes confirmed it.

Beneath him, in ragged caravan, were what he judged as a thousand men, and likely women too, though distinguishing details, despite his Swarovski Habicht glasses, from the height he was above them and the speed at which the helicopter moved was all but impossible.

For them to open fire on a Soviet helicopter was brazen indeed.

Texas was about to boil over.

Other intelligence reports seemed to indicate that some of the larger Brigand bands had been defeated by the Texas Volunteer Militia—and that some of the Brigand leadership had been swayed to the cause of the Resistance, further swelling the ranks of fighters in Texas and Eastern New Mexico for a land war against the Soviet forces.

Rozhdestvenskiy put down his binoculars and closed his eyes—almost sorry for them.

But in a way not.

It was the intent of valor, not the result, that measured bravery. That these people contemplated massive coordinated resistance was enough—that they would never live to bring their plans to fruition was not to diminish them.

"Can we go faster, captain?" Rozhdestvenskiy asked his pilot. It was nearly two in the afternoon in the central time zone, to which his new watch—a Rolex Datejust President—was set. There had been a fine jewelry store in Chicago on what had been State Street—and in the course of opening their vault, one of his men had discovered the wristwatch and presented it to him.

He smiled, wondering what other treasures—useless—the man had discovered and kept for himself that he had felt such guilt as to cavalierly give away a gold watch and its gold bracelet. Several thousand of the American dollars—useless, too, now, as opposed to diamonds, emeralds—what?

He supposed that afterward, if all proved out, if the massive experiment to which they were committed for their very survival proved successful, then perhaps diamonds would again have value beyond their gleam on the throat of a woman.

But he had prepared for that.

One secret convoy had been dispatched to The Womb—the gold taken from Fort Knox where the United States had held its gold depository.

It was unfortunate, but if he recalled correctly, DeBeers had had its American headquarters in New York City—and New York had vaporized on The Night of The War.

He was not callous enough, he realized, to merely regret the loss of all the diamonds. There were people, too. But now the diamonds might have more potential importance.

But that was a long time away—if ever at all.

And beneath, now, he saw the sprawling rubble of Houston, Texas—soon the Johnson Space Center, named after the American political leader and President. Soon the answer he sought.

It was, he laughed, however trite the thought, truly a matter of life and death. . . .

It had been an employee parking lot—it was obvious—but the Soviet officer on the ground, haggard-looking and tired, an army captain, had informed him of that anyway.

Surrounding the Johnson Space Center on all

sides were men of his Elite KGB Corps, once Vladmir Karamatsov's Elite Corps — but Vladmir, his friend, was no longer.

One platoon of army personnel had been admitted, along with the army officer through which all arrangements for penetration of the area had been arranged.

He was GRU — army intelligence. That meant that the man — he didn't remember the officer's name and it was better that way — might well place higher loyalty to General Varakov than to the KGB. All the men of his platoon were army intelligence as well.

The officer and his men would be eliminated — after the search of the Space Center had been completed.

It was necessary, Rozhdestvenskiy reflected, however unpleasant — however evil, and he knew it was that.

But if word leaked, to the army, to the Soviet people, who struggled to support the Asian land war — there could be mutiny, rebellion — and there was no time to deal with it.

No energy to spare for it.

Above the ground, the Johnson Space Center was in ruins — an earth mover groaned and grunted near the far corner of the building from the parking areas across which he strode beside the GRU officer.

Rozhdestvenskiy wore no uniform — a Harris tweed sports coat, a white button-down shirt open at the collar, his Single Action Army with his special loads under his coat. He appraised himself—the crease in his slacks neat, his Italian-made shoes polished to where they gleamed—having an orderly was a good thing.

"Captain—you are certain this machine will uncover the debris so we can enter below to the testing areas?"

"Yes, comrade Colonel—we have the plans to the structure—all is in readiness—much of the debris has already been moved and the stairwell can be seen. But work crews must precede us, comrade—that any dangers should be neutralized."

Rozhdestvenskiy moved his left arm, slapping it gently downward as his hand touched to the captain's shoulder. "I am indebted to you that there is such great concern for my safety, comrade—but I, too, am a soldier—we are accustomed to danger when the welfare of the state—of the people of the Soviet Union—when this is concerned."

Rozhdestvenskiy stopped, still some twenty yards from the noisy earth mover.

He lit a cigarette as the captain, the GRU officer, looked at him.

"Yes, comrade Colonel—all for the welfare of the people of the Soviet Union."

Rozhdestvenskiy smiled as he exhaled the smoke, the smoke caught up on the light breeze, dissipating rapidly.

He watched the GRU captain's eyes, then his own eyes shifted to the man's uniform holster at the waistbelt.

The GRU captain was a clever man.

As Rozhdestvenskiy stuffed his left hand into the pocket of his slacks, He slightly raised them — feeling the weight of the Colt Single Action Army on his belt. It was a reassuring weight. . . .

Flashlight beams streaked through the smoky darknesses as they marched ahead, played off partially collapsed ceilings, smoke-blackened tiles, off walls with gaping cracks in them.

Rozhdestvenskiy, ten of his own Elite Corps, and the GRU captain and three of his men.

Wide swinging doors off to his left — Rozhdestvenskiy pushed through them easily, slowly.

Beyond them, another laboratory — there were large horizontal silo-shaped objects — a Spacelab mockup, he guessed.

He let the doors swing shut.

They kept on, Rozhdestvenskiy's shoeshine ruined as he picked his way through the rubble.

He shot the flashlight beam to the face of the gold Rolex — they had explored the Space Center's cavernous underground for nearly two hours.

The dust penetrated his nose, he could feel it in his lungs — "Here! Comrade Captain! Here!"

It was one of the GRU men, shouting, waving his flashlight.

Rozhdestvenskiy broke into a loping run, leaping fallen debris like hurdles on an athletic field, his flashlight beam bouncing up and down, making bizarre zigzaggings on the far wall as he raced to be the first beside the army corporal.

Rozhdestvenskiy won the race—the captain a stride behind him, Rozhdestvenskiy turning his eyes to the corporal. The pale-faced boy stiffened, saluting, "Comrade Colonel—coffin-shaped objects are located inside this laboratory."

Rozhdestvenskiy gave the boy a salute, despite his own civilian clothes. It would be the boy's last salute.

He shoved through the doors, stepping inside. "Lights—all lights in here!" He commanded it, playing his own flashlight across the littered floor to the far side of the laboratory.

He counted them—twelve coffin-shaped objects—crates. They were stacked neatly near twelve smaller crates. The larger ones would be the chambers, the smaller ones the monitoring equipment.

He walked across the laboratory floor, footsteps loudly shuffling behind him, lights from flashlight beams silhouetting him against the crates now as he moved.

Rozhdestvenskiy stopped beside them.

Inside a wire cage were wooden containers, smaller still than either the chambers or the monitoring equipment. There were at least three dozen of them—perhaps more.

He drew his Colt, stepping back from the locking mechanism of the door of the wire grating enclosure. He fired the revolver, aiming for the lock.

The blast made his ears ring as it reverberated off the concrete walls.

He turned half left, kicking out with the sole of his right shoe against the lock — the door swung out, bouncing away from the cage as the locking mechanism clattered in pieces to the floor.

He crossed the threshold to the interior of the cage, the Single Action Army in his right fist, the flashlight in his left.

"More light — "

Between splits in the wooden packing cases, when he shone the light at the right angles, he could see inside — glass containers, perhaps three litres in capacity. Inside them a clear liquid with a slightly greenish tinge — reminiscent of Rhine wine.

He stepped back from the containers — the marking numbers on them stenciled in worn black paint.

"The Eden Project," he whispered — only to himself.

He turned, finding the GRU captain with his eyes, then raised the muzzle of his Colt .45. His right thumb jerked back the hammer, the captain turning to stare at him. "Comrade Colonel — but!"

Rozhdestvenskiy tripped the trigger, the top of the Captain's face exploding in chunks as the body seemed immobilized there for an instant.

Gunfire all around him now, Rozhdestvenskiy stepping back into the cage — shielding the containers with his body.

The gunfire stopped.

On the floor, at the center of the laboratory, his own men with guns drawn inspecting bodies, was the young corporal who had found the chambers, the monitoring equipment—and the precious liquid. The young corporal had sealed his own doom.

The body still moved, and Rozhdestvenskiy cocked the revolver again, firing it into the boy's head. The body stopped thrashing.

His ears ringing, the smell still fresh on the air in the dusty beams of the flashlight, he looked at his men. "Radio the surface—the others are to be eliminated. These crates—the large ones and the small ones, are to be carefully taken to The Womb by the most expeditious manner possible. These very small crates contain jars of liquid—it is the highest priority they reach The Womb immediately. If one is dropped and the contents damaged, one drop of the liquid lost—that man shall pay with his life—these are my orders."

Among the faces—some registering shock, he supposed—he found that of Lieutenant Gronstein—a good officer. "Lieutenant!"

"Comrade Colonel Rozhdestvenskiy!"

Rozhdestvenskiy looked at the younger man—then after an instant said, "This message goes to the bunker outside the Kremlin—to the command bunker—you have my codes—"

"Yes, comrade colonel."

"The Womb—The Womb shall receive its life."

He walked from the laboratory, stepping over

101

the body of the dead GRU corporal.

He felt mildly sick — but he would live now.

Chapter Twenty-seven

After extinguishing her last cigarette of the morning, Natalia had decided that whether she wanted it or not, she needed sleep, and a shower would only serve to keep sleep further out of reach. So instead she had removed her boots and stretched out on the couch underneath her fur coat — one of the few luxuries packed in the things she had brought with her from Chicago.

But a fur coat wasn't really a luxury — and after all, she had told herself, falling asleep under it, it was her uncle's secretary who had packed her things.

Paul Rubenstein still slept — and it was nearly evening. She marveled at his kidneys.

But she had watched the even rising and falling of his chest — he was well. She had been able to view the bandage — the wound to his left arm had not bled through.

She let him sleep — rest would help to cure him.

She had gone into the bathroom, brushed and flossed her teeth, brushed out her hair.

She had stripped away her black jumpsuit, her bra, her panties — Natalia stood now under the warm water of the shower, hair washed, washed again, conditioned, rinsed, rinsed again, re-rinsed, her body washed — soaking in the warmth.

She looked at the scar over her abdomen — like scars she had seen on other people, but never herself. It was a long, very thin scar — and she smiled, thinking Rourke, his hands on her, his scalpel cutting her, must have tried to make the scar as small as he could. It was reddish purple, and when it was completely healed, it would be like a tracing — of his fingertips.

And then she heard the noise from beyond the closed bathroom door. "Paul?"

No one answered her.

Naked, she stepped out of the shower and onto the bath mat, turning down the shower head with her right hand. "Paul?"

No one answered her.

She took the towel down — she had brought a fresh change of clothes into the bathroom and not a robe. There was no time to get dressed.

The first towel wrapped around her, barely covering her crotch when it was up enough to cover her breasts, she grabbed a second towel, ducking her head, wrapping the towel around her soaking wet hair turban fashion.

She raised her head, barefoot, stepping to the toilet, grabbing the two Metalife Custom L-

Frame .357 Magnum Smiths from the lid of the flush tank—the stainless steel guns were moist from condensation in the steamy air.

She stepped to the bathroom doorway, listening.

More sounds.

Holding one pistol under her left arm, she put her right hand to the doorknob, twisting it open.

But she left the door only slightly ajar.

The sounds of the inner door of the Retreat being opened or closed—she wasn't sure which.

Both revolvers in her hands, she stepped back from the door and kicked her bare right foot against the door, swinging it outward, fast.

As her right foot came down, she stepped a half-step forward on it, a wide, full step forward on her left leg, dropping down onto her right knee, the towel loosening as she moved, starting to slip, both pistols leveled, at eye level, in her clenched tight fists.

She moved her eyes.

A woman. A tall, handsome little boy. A pretty little girl with honey-colored hair.

John Rourke was visible coming from the storage area to the left of the main entrance and off the great room.

"Sarah—" Natalia whispered.

She suddenly realized the towel was going, reaching up her left hand, the revolver still in it, holding the gun across her breasts to keep the towel from falling.

The woman—about her own height, pleasant of figure, dark brown hair half obscured by a blue and white bandanna. The woman smiled, but a funny smile. She said, "You must be the Russian woman I've heard so much about—" and she started forward, down the three steps, across the Great Room as if she didn't see it, slowing, then coming up the three steps to the level of the bathroom. "I'm Sarah—John's wife," she smiled, taking the three steps quickly then, standing in front of Natalia. Natalia got to her feet, her left thigh pressed against her right, slightly ahead of it, her left hand with the revolver still holding the towel against gravity and her breathing. "So you are Natalia."

Sarah Rourke still smiled.

Natalia, her voice odd-sounding to her, answered. "Sarah—I wanted so to meet you. The children are beautiful."

"So are you."

Natalia didn't know what to say.

Chapter Twenty-eight

Michael and Annie had adopted Paul — he had awakened and appeared in the doorway of his bedroom a moment after Natalia and Sarah had met — Rourke had almost felt like kissing him, the distraction of his appearance breaking the tension between the two women. And the children had liked Natalia, as well.

With three bedrooms, the addition of three people had represented a logistical problem at the Retreat.

But Natalia had solved that. "Annie can sleep with me in my room, and Michael can sleep with Paul. That way, you and Sarah will have privacy — it's the best solution," and she had lit a cigarette.

Sarah had said nothing, only nodded agreement.

Annie had been ecstatic, and Michael — a more mature, more low-key child than Rourke had remembered him — had seemed enthused as well.

After they had explored the Retreat and

Rourke had used the microwave to make a hearty dinner that the children would like, there had been showers for Michael and Annie and then, both children weary, they had been put to bed.

Rourke stood beside his wife now, looking from the doorway at Annie, already asleep in Natalia's room, who seemed somehow lost in the king-sized bed. Michael was sleeping as well. Paul and Natalia sat on the couch in the Great Room, Natalia changed to a gray turtleneck knit top and black skirt, Paul wearing blue jeans with his shirt out of his pants.

Rourke had showered — he wore clean clothes, but clothes identical to what he always wore — except that he was without stockings and wore rubber thongs on his feet. He considered all that as he watched Sarah — he was a bland personality. He had always known that. In the days of civilization, when he had worn suits or neckties, his suits had always been conservative, his sports coats serviceable. He had early on realized that silk knit ties wrinkled less, lasted longer and were more comfortable about the neck. He had, consequently, used three neckties, replacing them with identical ties as needed — one blue, one brown, one black — all silk, all made in Italy, all knit, all identical in length and width — tying one was like tying the other. When a tie was given to him as a gift at a speaking engagement, or by one of the children for a birthday or Christmas, he had been perfunctorily grateful and hung the ties in the closet to gather dust and never be worn.

It was his way.

Sarah wore clothes Natalia had practically insisted that she borrow. Rourke had provided blue jeans, T-shirts, and sweaters in his wife's size in the stores for the Retreat, as well as underwear and track shoes and two pairs of combat boots. But Natalia had insisted Sarah would feel more at ease in more normal clothes. Rourke surveyed her, standing beside her—a pale blue blouse, a navy blue cardigan sweater——Sarah had complained the temperature in the Retreat seemed cold to her—and a blue A-line skirt. The skirt was longer than Sarah usually wore—but Natalia had always seemed more conscious of clothing than Rourke had ever found his wife to be. Incongruously, she wore a pair of the rubber thongs Rourke had stockpiled for her—black soled and not matching the rest of what she wore at all.

"What's the matter?" Sarah asked him.

"Just looking at you—it's good to be able to say that—just looking at you."

"I suppose I can always let Natalia borrow one of the three dozen pairs of Levis you stored here for me."

"I didn't know what to buy for you—you'd never even come up here."

"I'm not blaming you," she smiled.

He nodded, feeling himself smile at her as he let out a long sigh. "What do you say I buy you a drink, huh?"

"All right," and he watched the little dimples at the corners of her mouth deepen as she smiled up at him. "All right — I'd like that."

"Thanks for trying so hard — I mean — "

"Natalia seems like a good person — and I like Paul. But Natalia's in love with you — you know that, don't you?"

"Yeah."

"And you're in love with her — "

"I — "

"I didn't say you weren't in love with me — I know you are. I knew that wouldn't change. You love us both. And she knows that and so do I. Do you have any idea what's going to happen — to the three of us?" She leaned her head against his right shoulder, Rourke holding her left hand.

"You're my wife — and — "

"I know a lot about you, John — I always did. Sometimes, before The Night of The War, sometimes a friend would intimate that you were fooling around when you were away from me on those trips — "

"I never — "

"I always knew that — I never questioned it. Whatever happened between you and Natalia just happened — I guess that's why I can't be mad at her, either — "

"We, ahh — "

"I wouldn't have blamed you if you had — the children and I could have been dead. You looking for us like you did — finally finding us — that's an act of love no one in her right mind could argue with — dispute."

110

"I've told her this — and it's true — this was just something," he whispered, "something I didn't prepare for — do you know —"

"I know," and she leaned up to kiss him lightly on the mouth. "Natalia had that letter from her uncle that she wanted us to hear — and you promised me a drink — we can't settle anything now," and she squeezed his hand.

Rourke took her in his arms, kissing her hard on the mouth — he loved her. . . .

Rourke sipped at a glass of Seagrams Seven and ice, Natalia, Sarah, and Paul drinking the same. Rourke smoked one of his thin, dark tobacco cigars, Natalia smoking a cigarette — he wondered, absently, what it would be like for her when she ran out.

Natalia sat on the couch between Paul and Sarah, Rourke sitting in the reclining chair that flanked the coffee table opposite the couch.

Natalia opened the envelope. "It is addressed to you, John —"

He nodded, leaning forward, taking the envelope, his fingers touching hers as he took it.

Rourke sipped again at his drink. He looked at Sarah, "Natalia's uncle is General Ishmael Varakov, he's the supreme commander for the Soviet Army of Occupation in North America — but he's been straight with me the times I've had dealings with him — he's the head of the bad guys, you might say," and his eyes flickered to Natalia, watching the muscles at the corners of her blue eyes tighten slightly, "but an honorable man. He's a soldier doing his job — a patriotic

Russian — I can't fault him for that."

And then Rourke looked at the letter. It was dated some four weeks earlier.

He began to read, out loud.

"Doctor Rourke —

If you read this letter, Natalia, my niece, has arrived safely to your care. You may wonder that my English is so good — I spent many years in Egypt and in order to understand as much as I could, it was necessary to improve what English I already knew or master Arabic — the Egyptian variant, precisely. I had dealt with American and British officers during World War II and spoke English well enough to make myself understood — so I polished my English. I have sent Natalia to you not only for the reason which you suspect — that her position here deteriorates, as does mine. But another, more grave reason. You have heard, I'm sure, at least casual reference to something called The Eden Project — an American project done in cooperation with the NATO, SEATO, and Pan-American allies, but not with their full knowledge. It was a counter-measure to a post thermonuclear holocaust scenario, and this scenario is unfortunately coming to pass. When it transpires — very soon now — few if any living things will survive. What I offer to you, to the young Jew Rubenstein, and to your wife and children should you have located them by now, or find them still, is the slim hope of survival. It will in no way compromise your beliefs as a capitalist, nor my beliefs as a communist, if either dialectic can even matter. I offer this in exchange for your continued care of my niece, Natalia — like a daughter to me she has been all these years. I helped to raise her as the child of my dead brother and his wife, my brother a physician of great reknown, his wife a prima ballerina. I assume that you read this aloud to Natalia — if such is the case, help her to understand me when she learns this. For I had no brother at all, only two sisters who died during the early days of World War II. Natalia's father was indeed a physician of some great reknown —"

Rourke looked up — Natalia was staring, saying nothing, her eyes fixed —

". . . but a Jew. Her mother indeed was a ballerina — of the most incredible beauty and grace, her background Christian, and she was a practitioner of this religion despite the numerous injunctions of the State."

Rourke looked at Natalia again — Rubenstein held her left hand in his right.

". . . I was deeply in love with Natalia's mother — her name was Natalia too. But I learned—the original Natalia was as honest and decent a woman as is my Natalia, my niece—that she had secretly married Dr. Carl Morovitch, the Jewish physician. Considering myself a gentleman, I withdrew. But it was some years after the War—World War II, that Morovitch, himself only half Jewish, his mother's family name Tiemerov, spoke out against the oppression of Jews in the Soviet Union. I learned through my sources in GRU that his wife, Natalia, the woman I had loved, had departed the ballet before Morovitch's rash actions, which, had she been associated with them, would have forced her expulsion. And that Natalia was pregnant. I learned also that the KGB was plotting against Morovitch. I endeavored to warn Morovitch and Natalia—I still loved her, and she knew that I did. But they could not escape because Natalia was due to deliver her child. The child was born, a girl, longlegged and skinny, but with eyes the most beautiful blue color I had ever seen—except for the eyes of her mother. It was the father of my dead chauffeur, Leon, who accompanied me that night to the home outside Moscow where Morovitch and Natalia and the newborn child were in hiding from the KGB. Leon's father and I went there, because, through my GRU contacts, I knew the KGB was alert to their whereabouts. It was our intent—Leon's father was as loyal to me as Leon himself was — to spirit them away and get them to Finland and then to Sweden where they would be safe. We arrived too late—"

Rourke looked up, relighting his cigar — Natalia was weeping, Sarah's left arm around her shoulders. Rourke took a good swallow of his drink.

"—to save them. Doctor Morovitch had owned a gun — I had given it to him. He resisted the KGB as I too would have done. To defend his family. Carl Morovitch was dead, shot three times in the chest, then his throat slit. Natalia was bleeding and dying — one of the KGB officers was attempting to rape her. I shot him in the head — and then general shooting began. Leon's father was killed defending the small room Morovitch and Natalia had used as a nursery for the baby girl. I was shot in the leg — the left leg, and I still carry the bullet there. I could not trust a doctor to remove it at the time, and afterwards it became physically impossible to remove. But all the KGB were dead. The infant girl still lived. There was a woman — also once a dancer — whose services I used from time to time and whose discretion I trusted. I brought the infant to her. Through those few persons I trusted, with meticulous care, I altered my army records to indicate a brother who had lived with relatives ever since birth. This because of my family's poverty. I was a general by then, and the task was not as difficult as might be imagined. I found in recent death records a doctor who had no known family, a doctor named Plenko. It was not uncommon in the Twenties and Thirties to change one's name in Russia—it was sometimes necessity. To disguise criminal background or unfavorable political association. I made this man my brother. I invented of whole cloth a woman who was secretly his wife, but the name uncertain, and I invented her death. This too was simple enough. With parents for the infant girl, and myself established as her uncle, I acquired the house I still own on the Black Sea, esconcing the trusted woman there as my housekeeper—and to raise Natalia during my absence. For that is what I named her—Natalia, after her beloved, exquisite mother. The eyes gave me no choice, nor did my heart. And then Anastasia, because to me she was the lost princess—presumed dead. But my Anastasia was alive. Tiemerovna after her father's family. Two years later, the woman who was caring for Natalia married a doctor, his name Tiemerovitch, perhaps some distant relative of Morovitch's family. The woman and Tiemerovitch loved Natalia as their own. I once again altered my background records, eliminating the references to Dr.

116

Plenko and instead linking Dr. Tiermerovitch to myself as a lost brother. Tiemerovitch's medical career was greatly enhanced by the newly "discovered" relationship to a prominent Soviet general. I lied to Natalia only in that her "father" was my brother. After her father and mother—Tiemerovitch and his wife—died in an accident when Natalia was eighteen, again I took her in and saw to it that she had the best education, the best training. When she saw her patriotic duty as being linked to the KGB, I did not dare to interfere lest something somehow be suspected—and in times such as these, perhaps the greatest safety lies in being counted among those who threaten the safety of others. When she married Karamatsov, I was disheartened, but saw it as further enhancing her safety. Natalia—"my niece"—is all that I have, my obsession is that she live. Her mother died at the same age Natalia is now. I do not wish this for Natalia, whom I love."

"There is a choice for you. To save yourself, your friend, perhaps your wife and children, and since we both love her so deeply—"

Rourke licked his lips, looking at his wife, then looking at Natalia. He finished the letter, repeating the last few words—

". . . and since we both love her so

117

deeply, my niece. You must come to me in Chicago before it is too late — and bring Natalia with you, for there is no other way of it than to force her into danger again. I offer you the chance at life against certain death. Look to the skies, the electrical activity there each dawn — the End is Coming."

A scrawled signature was at the bottom of the note — the note itself was printed by hand.

Rourke folded the pages of the note together, setting down his cigar.

Natalia, her voice like he had never heard it, stood up, her fingers splayed along her thighs. "I will change to suitable clothes — my uncle —"

Rourke smiled at her, stood, walked around the table and folded her into his arms. "He loves you — and God help me, so do I —"

"I —"

"We'll leave as soon as you've changed." Still holding Natalia, he looked at Sarah's eyes. After all the years of marriage, the years of arguing, there was no argument there — but the understanding he had sought for so long.

He still held Natalia Anastasia Tiemerovna.

Chapter Twenty-nine

His weapons were laid out, his gear ready. They would ride double on his Low Rider to the place where they had left the prototype F-111, using that to get them to Chicago—it was the fastest way. Sarah stood behind him—he could feel her hands on his shoulders. He bent over to kiss Annie— "I love you, honey—honest," he whispered to her. She rolled over, not awakening, but a smile crossing her lips.

They left Natalia's room, Annie sleeping there, and moved on to Paul's room—Michael.

Rourke sat again on the edge of the bed. He looked at his son. He spoke to his wife. "If I die, Paul will care for you and the children. And pretty soon Michael will help him. Maybe he's too much like me—"

"He is," Sarah's voice murmured in the darkness.

"I tried," Rourke whispered, sighing loudly. "Honest to God, I tried. To be a father, a husband. If General Varakov is right—hell—" and he bent his head over his son, crying.

Sarah held his head—and in the darkness, she whispered, "I'll always love you—I hate your guts, but I'll always love you. I'll be with you if we all live or if we all die."

He swallowed hard, hugging his wife to him—and he let himself cry because he might never come home again. . . .

His sinuses ached as he strapped on the old holster rig for the Python. The belt was heavier, a spare magazine pouch with two extra-length eight-shot magazines for his .45s, the magazines made by Detonics. On the belt as well was a black-sheathed, black-handled Gerber MkII fighting knife with double-edged stainless blade with saw-teeth near the double-quillon guard on each side. He had the little Metalifed Colt Lawman in a special holster made by Thad Rybka for him years before The Night of The War—it carried the gun in the small of his back at a sharp angle.

He picked up the Government Model .45—a Mk IV Series '70, not the newer series '80 gun that had come out before The Night of The War. It, like the other two Colts he carried, was Metalifed. Chamber empty, the magazine loaded with 185-grain JHPs, he rammed the Colt into his trouser band.

The twin stainless Detonics .45s were already on him in the shoulder rig from Alessi, and the little Russell black Chrome Sting IA was in his belt.

The CAR-15 lay on the kitchen countertop. Beside it an M-16, one he had taken the time to hand-pick from the stores of weapons brought from the plane. Between the two assault rifles was an olive-drab ammo box, eight hundred rounds of 5.56mm Ball.

Beside him, as Rourke lit a cigar, was Paul Rubenstein, the younger man leaning against the counter. Rourke glanced at his friend — tired, worn from loss of blood. Rourke had inspected the wound — there had been little progress, almost none — but it was healing, and with the reduced level of activity would heal completely, he felt.

"I still say — "

Rourke looked at Rubenstein again. "No. With that wound — well, you know. But even if you didn't have the wound, I'd leave you here. Who the hell is gonna take care of Sarah and Michael and Annie for me? There's no one else I'd trust if there were somebody else around."

"So it's you and Natalia against whatever the hell her uncle's throwing you at?"

Rourke chewed down on his cigar. "Yeah — I guess that's the way of it."

"If you — "

"Don't come back — I can't tell you what to do. You're the best friend I ever had — in some ways, I guess, maybe the only one. You do what you think is best and it'll be the best — it sounds stupid to say it, but I have faith in you — I really do," and Rourke looked at his friend and smiled. . . .

It had taken Natalia long to change, he realized. She appeared from the bathroom wearing what John Rourke had come, subconsciously, to consider her battle gear — a tight-fitting black jumpsuit, nearly knee-high medium-heeled boots, the double-flap holster rig on her belt with the L-

121

Frame Smiths bearing the American Eagles engraved on the barrel flats. He could see the guns as she opened each holster in turn and checked the cylinders, then reholstered the revolvers and resecured the holster flaps.

As she walked across the Great Room, he saw that she too wore additional armament — the COP Derringer was not to be seen, but the little four-barreled .357 Magnum would be in her purse — the massive black canvas bag she almost invariably carried. But on her belt was a Gerber Mk II, the sheath apparently specially made, black, efficient-looking, the knife's handle material and the brass double-quillon guard betraying it as the Presentation series variation — just as efficient as the more subdued-looking Gerber Rourke now wore, but prettier.

She wore a shoulder rig he had never seen before — not something designed for concealment, but a field rig. Under her right armpit was a small black-handled knife, hanging upside down in a black leather sheath — he guessed a Gerber Guardian, the tiny boot knife similar in size to his Sting IA. Under her left armpit, balancing the rig, was what he recognized as a stainless steel Walther PPK/S, hanging upside down like the knife, protruding through the upside of the holster a stainless steel-looking — it could have been some type of aluminum — silencer, perhaps six inches long and the approximate diameter of a silver dollar. She saw him looking at it — "I had the silencer specially built — aircraft aluminum but very strong. The baffles need changing after every five hundred rounds or so—there's no slide lock, but I had the recoil spring altered so it functions perfectly with subsonic ammunition. It's very quiet that way—almost like a whisper. But with the regular recoil spring, like I have in it now, it handles 95-grain Hollow Points and it sounds about like a belch. I tested it a lot, but never used it in the field. In case we need a relatively silent shot, this should do it."

He saw Sarah looking at him—she stood beside Natalia.

He walked over to the two women, his right arm around Sarah, his left around Natalia. He drew both women close. There was no need to say what he felt.

Chapter Thirty

Natalia behind him, they had ridden in silence on Rourke's machine to the hidden aircraft. Like Rourke, she had carried two assault rifles, but both of hers were M-16s. As they worked now to remove the camouflage netting from the prototype F-111, she spoke. "What will you do, John?"

"About what your uncle has to tell us?"

"No—about Sarah and about me?"

"I don't know."

"You love her—and she loves you—it's plain to see for—"

"She said the same thing about you," Rourke said, stopping what he was doing, looking at her. "That she could tell I love you, and that you love me."

"And what did you say to her—if I can ask?"

"I told her—well, I guess pretty much what I told you." He chewed down hard on his cigar. "Paul is a fine man."

He watched her eyes in the darkness—another day was coming soon, the horizon pink with it in the east, chain lightning crackling across the sky there.

"Is that what you want—for me, for him?" Natalia asked, turning away from the plane, lighting a cigarette for herself.

"No," Rourke sighed. "I'm just saying it."

"This is a strange situation, John—silly, sad—all at once. If you had met me before you'd met Sarah, and then met Sarah later, I think we'd be talking about the same thing, wouldn't we?"

Rourke looked back at the fuselage of the jet. He nodded. "Yeah."

"I learned some things about myself tonight—when you read my uncle's letter."

"Look—"

"No—let me finish."

Rourke nodded only, lighting his cigar with the battered Zippo that bore his initials—he turned it over in his hands, feeling the engraving for the initials under his thumb. "So say it."

"How much my uncle loves me—it doesn't matter that he isn't really my uncle—he is my uncle. And Paul—I don't know how it feels to be a Jew, but I am one—half, at least. The way he reached out and held my hand when you read that part of my uncle's letter. And Sarah—she felt for me, about my mother and father dying. My uncle had always told me it had been an accident."

"You never checked?"

"I never saw any reason to—I guess that I was naive."

Rourke walked over to stand beside her, finding her left hand in the darkness, holding it tight.

"And about you—I learned a lot about you," she whispered. "That you really love me the same way you love her. That I could be a wife, a mother—that because of what I am and what I did sometimes—that—"

Rourke held her against his chest in the darkness.

It was insane. General Varakov had spoken as though the world would end. The lightning tracked across the sky.

But his only thought was that he loved two women—he realized now—equally.

Chapter Thirty-one

Sarah Rourke watched the man she had just met—he was younger than she, she guessed. She fixed a drink for him—Seagrams Seven and ice—and a drink for herself. Her husband's taste in liquor was as exciting and varied as his taste in women's clothing. If someone at the Retreat didn't like blended whiskey—and it was her favorite blended whiskey—they were out of luck.

"Good thing you're not a Scotch drinker," she called out to Paul Rubenstein, forcing a smile.

"Yeah—good thing," he nodded.

He was sitting in the sofa in what she had learned was called the Great Room. As she picked up his drink and her own, she sipped at hers briefly, studying the kitchen. "A microwave oven—God," and she felt herself smile. It would be good to cook again. Really cook.

She left the kitchen, walking down the three steps into the Great Room, setting Paul's drink down in front of him on the coffee table on a coaster, then sitting down at the farthest corner of the couch from him. She tucked her legs up under her, tugging at her borrowed skirt, smoothing it over her thighs—thinking about the woman to whom it belonged. The label in it was a label she had never even considered affording before The Night of The War. And the woman—she rode with her husband through the night, to do something or other that Sarah didn't quite understand. She sipped at her drink again. Paul Rubenstein seemed nervous to her.

"Is there something wrong?"

He looked at her, pushing his wire-rimmed glasses up on the bridge of his nose—it seemed more than a nervous habit with him—a preoccupation.

"No, Mrs. Rourke."

"It's Sarah, Paul—call me Sarah, please."

"Sarah," he nodded, picking up his drink, taking a swallow of it.

"There's something bothering you—is it that John left you here to stay with us and —"

"He couldn't have taken me the way my arm is — no. That just happened. It's not his fault—so I guess —"

"But there's something bothering you," Sarah insisted. As she moved her right hand, setting her drink down on a coaster on the end table nearest her, she saw the picture of herself and the children on the far side of the couch. Near Paul Rubenstein. She remembered when the picture was taken—they had just—

"I, ahh—" Rubenstein began, interrupting her thoughts.

"What?"

"I gotta talk—I shouldn't, ahh—" and he exhaled loudly—too loudly. It was as though something were bottled up inside him and just about to escape—she waited, listening, as she moved her hand back from her drink suddenly aware of the fact that for the first time in—how long?—she wasn't wearing a gun, she was wearing a skirt. She sat on a comfortable couch, in a secure place.

"I think we're going to be friends, Paul—the children really seemed to take to you. And I think—well—I think, so did I—you can tell me—sometimes just telling somebody is—"

He stood up—too quickly she guessed, because she saw him touch at his left arm as he walked behind the couch and stood beside the glass-front gun case—there were empty spots in the case now. All she could hear was the water as it spilled down the falls at the far end of the Great Room and into the pool there. She had no idea where it came from, or where the excess water went, because the pool seemed less than three feet deep—a mother always checked the depth of water her children would be playing near.

Paul Rubenstein started to talk then. "Before I met your husband," and his voice sounded slightly breathless to her, pain perhaps, but maybe not his arm. And his words were very hurried. "Well—I was just riding a desk in New York City. I had a girl—but New York isn't there anymore and neither is she. And I guess—shit—" and he turned around and stared at her, his eyes wide. "If what Natalia's uncle talked about is right—and maybe the world ends but somehow we just go right on living — what the hell am — " he turned away, her last glimpse of his face showing her that he seemed to be biting his lips, almost physically holding something back.

"That you'll be lonely," she whispered. "I know that feeling, Paul. John has me and he has Natalia and you have no one."

He looked back at her, saying nothing. She watched his eyes.

There was nothing she could say. She closed her eyes.

Chapter Thirty-two

General Ishmael Varakov sat at his desk in his office without walls amid the splendors of the museum. He stared at the mastodons from the distance.

Two extinct creatures fighting each other in death.

He shook his head slowly.

Reports.

No trace of Natalia or of the American Rourke, or of the young Jew who had accompanied Natalia. As if all three had disappeared from the face of the earth.

He felt a smile cross his lips — an ironic smile, he thought.

His feet hurt, and shoeless under his desk, his toes wiggled.

Reports.

There was no trace of the American Rourke's wife and children either. Clandestinely, Varakov had been searching for them for weeks, as further inducement to Rourke — and because it was the decent thing, he supposed.

Reports.

Karamatsov's ghost, Rozhdestvenskiy, had succeeded at the Johnson Space Center. Varakov's agent inside the KGB had verified that Rozhdestvenskiy had recovered what was presumed to be the serum and twelve of the American chambers. The American chambers could be compared to the Soviet chambers, the Soviet chambers modified if necessary. The serum, if Varakov understood the way of it, would be enough for thousands.

Reports.

All available army units were being mustered to a central staging area near the Texas-Louisiana border. A final battle with the surviving forces of U.S. II, but not for victory, for slaughter. But not even for that, he realized—simply to keep the army preoccupied, lest the true nature of The Womb be discovered and the horrible, final deception that it constituted.

Reports.

The small band of GRU and army personnel whom he trusted were in place, waiting. They did not know the mission, nor did they know the purpose. But to activate them without his niece and without the American Rourke would have been useless.

They might wait, never activated, until the End.

He stood up, heavily, slowly.

He began to stuff his feet into his shoes, watching Catherine as she slept curled up in the leather chair beside his desk. She had wanted to be with him, because dawn had been coming.

But dawn had come and gone.

And they both lived, at least for another day.

He began to walk, his feet hurting him badly because he had slept so little, rested so little.

He walked to his figures of the mastodons, studying them as he did in the museum's shadows. The building was nearly deserted. Some army functionaries, some KGB to keep Rozhdestvenskiy posted as to his — Varakov's — actions.

Nothing more. Soon, nothing at all.

He looked at the battling giants, battling in death. "Marx was right about history," he whispered in the darkness.

Chapter Thirty-three

Colonel Nehemiah Rozhdestvenskiy stood in the unopened doorway of the commandeered Lear executive jet, staring through the porthole in the pressure door at the airfield and beyond it Cheyenne Mountain — The Womb.

The Lear finally stopped its movement under him, settled as he peered out on the central elevator pad. And a new sensation of movement began — lowering.

There was brilliant sun like a halo around the field as he stared through the porthole, then a flicker of darkness, shadow, and then the brilliance of artificial, more yellow light.

The copilot was suddenly beside him, working the controls to open the door, the door pushing outward, passenger stairs folding out automatically, before him as the down motion stopped.

Commander of the North American Branch of The Committee for State Security of the Soviet, Colonel Nehemiah Gustafus Rozhdestvenskiy — he was keenly aware of who he was, what he was — looked to his blue-black uniform's left shoulder—the green shoulder board bearing the triangular formation of three stars denoting him as full colonel, KGB, had a speck of dust on it. He flipped it away with his white-gloved right hand.

Before stepping outside—the band already playing the national anthem—he glanced at himself in the lavatory door mirror near the exit.

His nearly knee-high black jack boots gleamed with the richness of their leather and the labor of his aide. The brass of his buttons and the buckle of his gold parade dress uniform belt caught the overhead lighting, sparkled. His medals—not all of his medals, for to wear them all would have shown a lack of taste, something he despised in others of his rank or above, something he detested in men beneath his rank—followed the line of his left lapel, plunging in a sharp angle from the uniform above his left breast toward his belt. The red collar tabs high on his lapels, the redness of the wide band that encircled his uniform cap—he adjusted the angle of his cap to where it dipped slightly over his left eye.

Rozhdestvenskiy turned from the mirror, glancing neither to right nor to left, stepping through the doorway, standing on the top step of the egress, raising his right hand in salute, the voices of the assembled troops raised in chorus, his own joining their voices: *"Soyuz nerushimy respubliks-vobodnykh. . . ."*

The hammer and sickle—he stared at it as it waved in the breezy downdraft from the elevator opening above him.

The men—their uniforms worn proudly, the

7.62mm Kalashnikov rifles with bayonets fixed held at high port across their chests, all eyes turned as the men—more than a thousand strong—all looked at his face.

Still holding his salute as the strains of the Soviet national anthem died, he turned fully to face his troops.

Smartly—so they would know how he meant it—he snapped away the salute—to them.

Rozhdestvenskiy descended the steps, Major Revnik, his executive officer, striding forward, saluting as he called out in stentorian tones, "The troops are assembled, comrade colonel!"

Rozhdestvenskiy returned the salute smartly, starting forward, Revnik falling in step to his left.

Faces—young, healthy, strong, dedicated. Men. And ranked behind them, in white blouses and black skirts with red neckerchiefs tied at the throats of their blouses, were the women. A thousand strong as well—the finest and best and strongest and most beautiful.

The men, armed, ready, the women—all were ranked in identical formations on both sides of him as he walked the length of the underground hangar bays of what once had been North American Air Defense Headquarters—NORAD.

Now, The Womb.

Tanks—the massive T-72—ranked endlessly beyond them as far as he could see.

In the distance, he viewed the generating equipment for the particle beam weapons that formed their air defense and that would make them ultimately masters of the earth.

Standing at the far end of the ranks as he walked, in the exact center, was a solitary young woman. In her arms was a bouquet — roses, he thought.

He walked toward her, seeing her face, her flowing black hair — her eyes were dark, her figure exuding the radiance of health.

Rozhdestvenskiy stopped.

The woman stepped toward him.

"Comrade colonel — the loyal women of the Soviet Union who have been honored by their selection to perpetuate forever the noble spirit of the triumphant peoples of the State salute you!"

She handed him the bouquet. She leaned up and kissed his left cheek and his right cheek.

Revnik's voice: "To the triumph of the Soviet!"

Two thousand voices shouted, the halls ringing with it — "Triumph!"

Chapter Thirty-four

Rourke was awake, having slept while Natalia flew, and as he sat up in the copilot's seat, he could watch the ground below them — at treetop level they were coming in. "John — your restraint —"

Rourke checked the lap and shoulder harness — it was secure.

He watched her hands as they played over the instruments, then looked away, watching through the plexiglass — the treetops were now even with them as the jet skimmed over a fence, Natalia already throttling back — he could hear it — as she committed them to landing.

It was a small country airstrip — but the runway surface in good shape as he watched its grayness seeming to swallow the forward view, rising up in a blur of roughness and bleakness — and he felt the impact of touchdown, hearing the skidding, hearing and feeling as Natalia throttled down.

Into his microphone, he whispered, "You're a fine pilot."

"Now is a poor time to verify that, isn't it," her voice came back. . . .

There was no chance to land the plane somewhere where it might not be detected—and so the plane, Rourke considered, was written off. Speed in reaching Varakov was the ultimate concern and the small airfield just north of the Illinois-Wisconsin line was the closest thing his map had shown and small enough, he had hoped, that there would be no Soviet guards.

So far, as they left the plane in the field, as they walked, their assault rifles ready, no guards were in evidence.

"We will steal a car?"

"If we can—you can always try your Soviet I.D. and see if you can convince them you arrested me—"

"I do not think I would find greater favor now with the KGB than would you, John—"

Rourke only nodded. Fifty yards still until the edge of the airfield, fifty yards of exposure still. As if reading his thoughts, Natalia said, "When I made the overflight—before I awakened you—there was nothing."

"Can't always tell from the air," he cautioned. They had left the plane without a booby trap, no time really to construct one. One additional jet fighter for the Russians would not sway the odds in even the most minute way, he had reasoned, and perhaps leaving it here some Resistance unit would find it and make use of it.

They were passing an outbuilding, made of corrugated metal, Rourke's eyes flickering toward it. "Run for it," Rourke shouted, shoving at Natalia, sweeping the M-16's muzzle toward the building. Something—he didn't know what—

"Halt!"

The voice was from his right, and he wheeled toward it, squinting in the sunlight despite the dark-lensed glasses he wore. A single man, holding what looked from the distance to be a Ruger Mini-14.

Natalia was swung toward him, her M-16's muzzle leveled at his midsection.

Rourke stepped beside her. In his left hand he carried the eight-hundred-round ammo box of 5.56mm ball, in his right hand he clenched the M-16. "What do you want?" Rourke challenged.

"Who the hell are you people—with that plane?"

"I work for the F.A.A.—checking out rural airports—"

"Knock it off," the solitary man with the Ruger rifle called back. At the corners of his peripheral vision, Rourke could see more armed figures—men and women—stepping out from inside the building, coming from the far edge of the field.

"I don't like this, John," Natalia whispered hoarsely.

Rourke said nothing, watching only.

The man with the Mini-14 spoke again. "Who are you?"

"I'm John—this is Natalie—who the hell are you?"

"Morris Dumbrowski — Combined Counties Resistance Fighters."

Rourke breathed a long sigh. "Then relax — we're on the same side."

Then a woman's voice, from his right, near the corrugated metal building's door.

"I've seen her — she's the one who was always with the general — the one in the fur coat — maybe his slut or something!"

Natalia wheeled toward her, Rourke stepping between Natalia and the woman. "No," he snarled to Natalia.

"I'm not his woman — I'm his niece," Natalia shrieked.

Rourke rasped under his breath, "Shit —"

"Russians — fuckin' Commies!" It was Morris Dumbrowski's voice, Rourke turning to face the man.

"I seen her," another woman's voice shouted. "She was with that bastard who used to run the KGB — maybe she's his woman."

Natalia wheeled toward the new voice, shouting, almost screaming, "I was his wife — and he's dead — he was a butcher!"

Rourke stepped beside Natalia. "My name's John Rourke — if you're Resistance like you say you are, you must know Colonel Reed — get in touch with him at U.S. II headquarters — he can vouch for us both."

"Why?"

Rourke turned to face the voice — it was the woman from the corrugated building — she was walking toward them, holding a pistol, some kind of double-action revolver with a barrel that looked too long to be comfortably carried. She kept talking. "So you can get your Commie friends to get a fix on our radio, or maybe get a fix on U.S. II? Fuckin' rot in hell, mister—"

"It's not mister," Natalia said, Rourke shocked by the calm suddenly in her voice. "It's Doctor—he's a doctor of medicine, and I'm a major in the KGB—but if the KGB were to find me, they'd likely kill me. General Varakov—he is my uncle, and we go to see him—he is helping to fight the KGB."

"You're crazy, lady—and if he's a doctor, then he's your psychiatrist," the woman with the long-barrel revolver from the corrugated building laughed, the laugh almost a cackle.

"Then I will kill you," Natalia said. "It is not Natalie, my name—it is Natalia Anastasia Tiemerovna, major, Committee for State Security of the Soviet. I have told the truth." Natalia raised her M-16, the rifle in both hands, her legs spread wide apart, the muzzle of the rifle aimed at the woman with the long-barreled revolver.

Rourke rasped, "Contact Colonel Reed—and take a look at this—I'll move slow." Rourke reached to Natalia's right holster, opening the flap there, the M-16 swinging free on its sling, the CAR-15 across his back. He set down the ammo box, taking the second revolver from the holster on Natalia's left hip.

He heard someone cock a weapon in the crowd of Resistance fighters.

Rourke rolled both revolvers in his hands,

butts forward, walking toward the woman with the long-barreled revolver, walking slowly.

The woman looked down at his hands.

Rourke could feel Natalia's eyes boring into him.

Rourke stopped less than two feet from the woman with the long-barreled revolver—she was evidently one of the leaders, but not the first in command, he guessed.

Rourke held the perfectly matched .357s butts forward, showing the woman the twin revolvers. "The American Eagle on the barrel flat here of the revolver in my left hand. They were made for Sam Chambers by a guy named Ron Mahovsky, a company called Metalife Industries. Mahovsky—before The Night of The War—he was one of the top revolver smiths in the country. Sam Chambers gave these revolvers to her—to Natalia, Major Tiemerovna, because he didn't have a medal to give her. When the quakes hit Florida—you heard about that?"

The woman nodded.

"If it hadn't been for Major Tiemerovna, thousands more of American lives would have been lost—and President Chambers knew that. Take a look at these yourself," Rourke said, holding the revolvers out toward the woman, butts presented toward her. "And be careful, ma'am—they're loaded."

His eyes watched the woman's eyes. She looked at the guns Rourke offered her, at her own revolver—Rourke knew what it was now, a Smith & Wesson Model 10 M&P with six-inch barrel, just a .38 Special. The woman dropped the gun into a too small holster on her right thigh, the bottom of the holster cut out, two inches of barrel protruding through it.

She reached for both revolvers at once.

He'd seen his cowboy heroes do it in countless movies when he had been a boy.

He did it now — the road agent spin, edging his trigger fingers into the guards, letting the revolvers roll inward, away from his palms, snapping his hands up as the guns moved, the revolvers twirling on their trigger guards, both gun butts dropping into his fists, his thumbs working back the hammers instinctively — he had practiced the trick with single-action semi-autos, used it a time or two — and both pistols moving, Rourke himself moving.

He was beside the woman, slightly behind her, the pistol in his left hand, its muzzle finding the underside of her chin, ramming up against the flesh, the gun in his right hand at the side of her body, pointed at the man with the Mini-14, Morris Dumbrowski — Natalia had wheeled, her M-16 pointed toward the Resistance fighters who had come from the far side of the field.

It had taken perhaps a second, and Rourke, his voice loud, shouted, "She gets it first, and then you Dumbrowski — I'm telling the truth, so's the major — take us to Resistance headquarters and a radio and Reed will back us up, or Chambers himself."

"You telling us —" Dumbrowski began. "You

tellin' us, that you've got some kinda mission—that U.S. II—"

"U.S. II didn't send us—my uncle sent for us," Natalia called out. "But he's a decent man. There is something gone wrong—something wrong for all of us—and he thinks that Doctor Rourke and I can do something to stop it—that is why we come here."

"And we could use your help—the Resistance's help—getting into the city—to get to him."

The woman Rourke held in his arms, the woman he held a gun to, coughed, saying, "You want us to help you reach General Varakov?"

"It's the only way—maybe. What's it going to be—we all shoot each other here and now for nothing, or you check out our story?"

"Throw your guns down then," Dumbrowski shouted.

"We keep our guns—no other way," Rourke shouted back.

It was the woman—Rourke had been wrong—who was the leader. She raised her voice, shouting across the field, "Put your guns away—but keep an eye on both of them—we're going to the base," and her hands came up, touched at the barrel of the revolver under her chin and gently, slowly, moved it aside.

Rourke let go of her, the woman turning to face him. "I'm Emily Bronkiewicz—our leader was killed three weeks ago—I was his wife. I'm the leader now. Stay with us, close, or we'll open fire."

145

And her eyes drifted to the revolver in Rourke's left hand, the gun held diagonally away from him. "You were right about the American Eagle—but now let's see if the guns were really a gift—and if you're telling the truth, we'll help if we can. If you're not, then go ahead and shoot me when you want to—but there're enough of us to get both of you."

Rourke lowered the hammers on both revolvers—slowly.

He walked past the woman, to give Natalia her guns back. He whispered to the Resistance leader, "Don't bet on that last part."

Chapter Thirty-five

The base to which Emily Bronkiewicz had referred was at first look a cave dug out of a sloping hillside, Rourke and Natalia in the middle of the Resistance group, walking stooped over through the cave by flashlight beam, a brighter light ahead, noise as well.

The tunnel abruptly stopped, Rourke suddenly realizing he could stand to his full height, Natalia rubbing the small of her back with her hands as she did likewise.

The tunnel had ended in a building, a structure largely concrete with heavily shuttered high windows—or at least Rourke assumed them to be windows—and double steel doors at the far end. The building seemed nearly a perfect square, drill presses—dust covered—and lathes and other machinery in evidence, as though pushed aside into corners of the building, the floor oil-stained in spots, large patches of it, gummy-looking as Rourke and Natalia followed Emily Bronkiewicz across the floor, diagonally toward a cubicle-style office at the height of a dozen or so stairs that overlooked the main floor.

Rourke surmised that it had once been a plant manager's office, the place apparently at one time a machine shop. Its exact nature was hard to determine.

Others of the Resistance broke off before reaching the stairs, Rourke and Natalia continuing to follow Emily Bronkiewicz.

She started up the steps, Natalia immediately behind her, Rourke following Natalia, Dumbrowski and two other men behind Rourke.

Emily paused at the office door, turning the knob, opening the door inward.

Natalia followed her inside, Rourke after Natalia, only Dumbrowski coming inside after Rourke.

Emily perched herself on the front edge of the gray metal desk at the rear of the office.

Natalia remained standing.

Rourke shrugged, sitting down in the metal interview chair and pushing it away from the side of the desk, turning out to face Emily Bronkiewicz. "So — where's the radio?" Rourke asked her.

"I'm a Pole, Dr. Rourke — if that's your real name."

"It's really Rourovitch and I'm a spy."

Emily looked at him, but didn't smile. "I hate the Russians. I hated them before The Night of The War, for what they did in Poland. My oldest son — he was thirteen. He got killed fighting the Russians. My husband just died. Doing the same

148

thing. My daughter's in such a way that she won't even talk. She's seventeen—a Soviet soldier. He was drunk, he raped her. She caught something from him—some kind of disease. But we don't even have penicillin to fight it. My mother and father lived in Chicago—they died during the neutron bombing on The Night of The War. My husband's brother was arrested and hauled away to a forced labor camp or something—"

"A factory," Natalia interrupted. And Emily Bronkiewicz looked at her. "It would have been a factory. There are no forced labor camps here—but the laborers at the factories are not allowed to leave—so it is like a camp. They are fed well—it was my uncle who insisted that they work in eight-hour shifts only and be treated decently."

"Is that your excuse?" the woman asked.

"It is not an excuse—it is merely the truth."

"They made him a slave—that's simple enough to understand. He has to work for them, can't come back. I don't know where he is, even if he's still alive at all."

"What are you trying to say?" Rourke asked the woman.

"Out there on the airfield—well, you could have killed a lot of us. Here—no such luck for you. I've got all my people outside. If I don't step outside with you two following me, you'll never get out of here alive. First gunshot they hear, they'll be ready, and if I don't come out, they'll come in and kill you. Shoot the walls out

149

of the office here to kill you both. But kill you — kill you anyway. Me — I don't matter much no more anyway."

Morris Dumbrowski swept the muzzle of his Mini-14 up, fast, Rourke starting to move, Natalia's right hand flashing across her body, the silenced stainless Walther in her right fist.

Rourke shifted direction, going for Emily Bronkiewicz, his right hand bunched into a fist, flashing out toward her jaw as he came out of the chair.

He heard something that sounded like a loud belch, the mechanical noise of a slide moving out of battery, back into battery, the clatter of metal against wood. Rourke's fist found Emily Bronkiewicz's jaw, a light tap to throw her off balance, his left hand reaching out across her body and smothering her right as she made to draw her long-barreled revolver.

As Emily slumped back, Rourke's hand moved up to cover her mouth, Dumbrowski starting to say something, but Rourke heard Natalia cut him off, "Shh."

Rourke had the Bronkiewicz woman, supporting her from falling off the desk, her revolver out of the leather in his left fist, pointed at the woman.

She moaned, Rourke watching as her eyelids fluttered.

He could hear Natalia talking, her voice a whisper. "I could have just as easily killed you, Mr. Dumbrowski — but I only shot you in the right forearm — that'll heal."

"You'll never—"

"Shh—"

The door from the head of the steps outside the office started opening, Natalia sidestepping, Rourke leaning Emily Bronkiewicz back roughly across the desk, beside the door in two strides, the first man coming through the doorway. Rourke hammered down with the barrel of the ungainly sized M&P revolver, his wrist taking the impact as ordnance steel impacted bone, the man slumping forward.

Rourke let him fall, starting for the second man, his shotgun starting to swing on target, his mouth opening to shout, Rourke reaching for him.

There was a flash of something, something gleaming, catching light as it moved, the man's mouth open but not making noise as the man's eyes shifted right, fast. Rourke stepped into the man, shoving the riot shotgun's muzzle hard to the man's right, Rourke's right fist hammering out, tipping against the base of the man's jaw, the head snapping back.

Rourke started to catch the body as it sagged, glancing once at Natalia, the stainless silenced PPK/S shifted into her left hand. He looked at the door—the man's right arm was pinned there by the Bali-Song, the handle slabs open and spread, the Wee-Hawk pattern blade penetrated through the leather of the man's jacket and at least a half-inch into the soft wood of the door.

Rourke wrenched the knife free, dragging the

body through the doorway, then easing the door closed.

He stood beside the doorway, "You throw a good knife, Natalia," Rourke told her, looking up from the knife, closing it, locking the handle slabs together, then tossing the Bali-Song to her.

She caught it in her right fist, making it disappear into a pocket of her black jumpsuit. "Pacific Cutlery made a good knife — all I did was practice a lot," and she smiled.

"You two Commies quit congratulatin' yourselves — you ain't never gettin' outa here alive."

It was Dumbrowski, and Rourke looked at the man.

Rourke picked up the man's Mini-14 from the floor. He examined the gun — stainless steel, factory folding stock, factory twenty-round magazine in place.

Rourke turned the gun around and handed it to Dumbrowski.

"If we're here to do you harm, why haven't we killed any of you? Natalia's shot could have put out your lights, Natalia's knife could have killed the man at the doorway. How come? Enemy agents and we don't like to kill? That make sense to you? Now where's the goddamned radio, Dumbrowski — call U.S. II and we can quit this idiocy."

It was Emily Bronkiewicz's voice — Rourke hearing it from behind him.

"We don't have no radio here — "

There was gunfire suddenly — heavy caliber assault rifle fire.

"Those are Kalishnikovs," Natalia almost hissed, turning away from Dumbrowski. "Some of my people — perhaps the plane was spotted."

"Fuckin' Commie trick," Dumbrowski shouted.

Rourke punched Dumbrowski in the mouth, hammering him down into the interview chair.

Rourke looked at Emily Bronkiewicz. "What you said makes sense," she nodded. "We can talk later — let's get the hell out of here."

Natalia had made the Walther return to its shoulder rig, both revolvers in her hands, the M-16s hanging from her sides. "I can't kill my own — "

There was a roaring sound then, cutting off her words, Rourke beside the windows of the office, then dropping away, shouting, "Hit the floor!"

The doors had been blown through, the floor of the office shuddering with the concussion. Rourke rolled, was up, his M-16 coming into his hands. Natalia, beside the desk, was helping Emily Bronkiewicz to stand — a shower of glass covered the desk — and the Bronkiewicz woman's left arm was slashed.

"Stop the bleeding," Rourke rasped, opening the door.

He recognized the uniforms, but more important, the technique — men poured through the blasted open doorways now, green shoulder boards on their brown uniforms — KGB. AKM flashed fire in their hands, the Resistance on the ground level of the machine shop holding them for the moment near the blown-out doors.

"Let's get out of here — down the steps — fast," Rourke ordered, jumping through the doorway. Dumbrowski was behind him, half dragging the semiconscious man Rourke had decked in the doorway.

Rourke looked back — Natalia and Emiliy Bronkiewicz, Emily's arm bandaged with a shirt-sleeve, helping the man Rourke had cold-cocked with the barrel of the revolver, the revolver back in Emily's right fist, Natalia's one revolver holstered, but her left hand still holding one as she shouldered half the weight of the man.

Rourke rammed the muzzle of his M-16 forward, throwing the assault rifle to his shoulder, firing down from the top of the steps toward the KGB invaders.

As he started down the steps, gunfire began pouring toward him, the sounds of what glass hadn't been blown out of the office walls in the explosion now shattering as stray rounds impacted it.

Rourke fired into the KGB invaders again, their knot beside the blown-open steel doors thinning as they drew back.

An officer — Rourke saw the man as he looked up. Rourke heard his shout — in Russian, which Rourke understood. "It is Major Tiemerovna — she is ordered to be killed!"

"Down," Rourke shouted back to Natalia. "Down, Natalia!"

Rourke made to fire the M-16 — a three- or

four-round burst and the rifle was emptied.

The Soviet officer was leading a group of a half-dozen men—they had broken through the Resistance fighters, were charging the staircase, the officer holding a pistol, the six men with him AKMs.

Rourke let the M-16 fall to his side on its sling as he took the stairs down two at a time, both Detonics pistols coming into his hands, his thumbs jacking back the hammers.

He discharged both pistols toward the center of mass of the charging KGB officer—once, then once more, the man's body falling back.

Four AKs were turning on him, Rourke taking a half-step back, his pistols raised.

There was a burst of assault rifle fire, then another and another, from the stairs above him.

Three of the Soviet soldiers went down, Rourke firing his pistols, emptying them toward the remaining three men, more assault rifle bursts—one an M-16 on full auto, the other only a semiauto—coming from behind him.

The last three men were down.

Rourke rammed both pistols into his belt, grabbing the Colt Mk IV already there, jacking back the slide. He looked up the steps—Natalia, and beside her Dumbrowski—and Emily Bronkiewicz was staring at her.

Natalia's face was ashen—Rourke read it in her eyes. She had killed her own.

As he turned away, raising the Colt, firing twice into the dissipating knot of KGB troops, he heard Emily Bronkiewicz shouting from the top of the stairs. "These two are on our side—make a run for the tunnel—quick!"

Rourke emptied the Metalifed Government Model .45, covering Emily, Dumbrowski, and the two other men—they moved well enough now—as they descended the stairs.

It was almost like moving someone in a trance as, his M-16 reloaded—he half dragged Natalia toward the tunnel.

Behind them was another explosion and more gunfire.

"Hurry!" Rourke rasped.

Chapter Thirty-six

Rourke and Natalia were the last two into the tunnel, except for Emily Bronkiewicz—she was lighting a fuse. "This'll stop the bastards—but good," she sneered. "Dynamite—and plenty of it—blow the whole damn place down on their fuckin' heads!"

She struck the match, set the fuse—it hissed.

KGB men were everywhere on the floor of the machine shop now, assault rifle fire heavy, Rourke dividing his attention between the men and reloading his guns. Without looking at Natalia, he murmured, "You all right?"

Her voice—lifeless. "Yes—I just never thought it would come to this—they had orders to kill me."

"I speak Russian, remember?" and he looked at her.

She only nodded. "But why kill me?"

Rourke shook his head, not answering.

"Why kill me?"

Rourke looked at her—it was impossible for him to imagine Natalia hysterical—but she was

157

near hysterics. "I don't know—maybe—maybe they found out some things—maybe your uncle did some things—and we won't know until we try to reach him—"

"Try?"

Rourke saw it in her eyes—fear, hatred. She raised her M-16, firing out a long burst toward the advancing brown-uniformed KGB.

The weapon was shot out. A moment's silence. The hissing of the fuse. He couldn't hear it. Then Emily Bronkiewicz, screaming— "The fuse—it's out!"

Rourke, stooped over, charged back the few yards down the tunnel, toward Emily Bronkiewicz. "Where's the dynamite?" Rourke demanded.

"Out there—back inside the mess of machinery—" and she gestured toward the drill presses and lathes Rourke had seen shoved aside earlier. Gunfire hammered toward them, Natalia beside Rourke, ramming a fresh stick up the well of her M-16.

Rourke shifted his box of .223 to the tunnel floor, staring through into the machine shop toward the piled-up machinery and the dynamite there. He couldn't see it to shoot at it, couldn't see where the fuse had stopped burning.

"Mrs. Bronkiewicz—take this box of ammo with you—if Major Tiemerovna and I get out of here, we'll need it." And Rourke looked at Natalia. "Cover me—I'm goin' for the dynamite."

"To kill yourself—that's fine, but I'm coming with you."

"Damnit—" Rourke shifted his M-16 forward, shouting to Emily over a burst of Soviet AKM fire, "Lay down some covering fire for us until we get up there—then run like hell."

Rourke started into the machine shop, running in a long-strided, low-silhouetted lope, his M-16 in one hand, his scoped CAR-15 in the other, firing both assault rifles, Natalia running beside him, Natalia—as he caught her at the edge of his left eye's peripheral vision—firing an M-16 in each hand.

There were two dozen assault rifles firing at them—Rourke made it, bullets ricocheting, zinging off the abandoned machinery, sparks of fire along the concrete floor, Rourke feeling something tear at the sling of the M-16.

He kept running, firing out the M-16, still firing the CAR-15. Natalia was ahead of him now, hidden in the mass of abandoned machinery, Rourke half diving down beside her as the CAR-15 ran dry, assault rifle fire pinging into the machinery, like a swarm of angry insects around their heads and bodies.

Rourke snatched one of the thin, dark tobacco cigars from the left breast pocket of his blue chambray shirt under the battered brown bomber jacket. He lit the cigar in the flame of the Zippo.

"Bad for your health," Natalia snapped, firing a burst from one of the M-16s, then tucking back down.

Rourke reloaded the M-16, then the CAR-15, working the bolt release almost simultaneously to chamber the first rounds in the guns. He left the safeties off.

He searched the pile of machinery—looking for the dynamite— "There—the fuse," he heard Natalia call to him.

Rourke looked to her eyes, tracked them, found the thin gray-white line of fuse running along the wall above their heads.

He tracked it forward, the fuse disappearing into the pile of machinery. He shoved aside a small metal platform, a cardboard box visible at the end of the fuse.

Sucking in his breath, inhaling deeply on the cigar—there was more gunfire around them—he backtracked the fuse—it had been cut—perhaps by a bullet, a chunk of the concrete wall dimpled there—midway between the sewer pipe opening into the tunnel and the machinery beside which he hid.

There was barely eight feet of fuse within his reach.

"What are we going to do?" Natalia asked, firing a burst from one of the M-16s. "They're closing in."

Rourke nodded, saying nothing, trying to think.

"If I pull down that fuse," he said finally, "I'll rip it out, maybe. And if I light it from here, we'll never make it through the tunnel before it blows—I've gotta get up there along the wall—near those shuttered windows—and then light the damn thing."

"You'll be killed—nobody could miss a target

160

your size profiled against the wall."

"A target my size—thanks a lot," and Rourke grinned at her.

He shifted off the M-16, leaving the scoped CAR-15, his personal weapon in more battles than he wanted to remember, slung across his back, handing Natalia the M-16. "Three of 'em now—just keep pumpin' lead toward those guys—keep me covered—and once I get that fuse lit, give a good loud scream and shout something about dynamite, then run like the devil's chasing you for the tunnel."

She leaned toward him, quickly, taking the cigar from his mouth, kissed him. "If we live, I don't know what will happen to us—but I love you, John Rourke."

He looked at her. Women picked the craziest times for things, he thought. Or maybe they didn't at all.

"I love you, too—I couldn't help it—and I'll always love you—now start shooting," and Rourke took back his cigar, looked at her once, then shot a glance toward the KGB out beside the blown-open metal doors, running for the near wall across the length of the machine shop.

There were crates there, and if they didn't collapse under his weight, he could stretch and just maybe reach the fuse—and he did what he had told Natalia to do. He ran as if the devil were chasing him, gunfire in a barrage surrounding him.

Chapter Thirty-seven

Natalia raised one of the three M-16s, firing out the entire magazine, zigzagging the muzzle over the positions of the KGB unit, dropping the empty assault rifle, firing three-round bursts as heads raised from the cover of the machine shop equipment, one three-round burst catching an enlisted man in the upper left side of his chest, blowing his body back, ripping his green shoulder board from his uniform tunic, a second burst slicing across the neck of another enlisted man, the third burst cutting the legs out from under an officer climbing over a packing crate, starting toward her across the no man's land between them.

She fired a fourth burst, three headshots in a rough diagonal from jawline to left eyeball, a marksman with an AKM — an enlisted man — leveling his rifle at Rourke, she guessed, no time to look, to confirm that the burst the man had gotten off hadn't killed the man she had loved since first seeing, the man she would always love.

Another three-round burst, against two men starting over some of the packing crates, hammering one man against the other. The machinery around her seemed to explode, a fusillade of automatic weapons fire making her pull back.

She changed the partially spent magazine in the rifle she held, reaching out for the fired-out M-16, the metal hot as the back of her left hand inadvertently brushed against the barrel, changing the magazine there as well.

She looked across the machine shop toward Rourke. He had taken cover near the packing crates beneath the faint thread of dynamite fuse.

Three rifles loaded and ready, Natalia rammed one of the M-16's up over the lathes and machinery around her, firing it blindly, blowing the magazine, careful not to use the same weapon she'd used the first time lest she burn out the barrel.

She rolled left, another fresh-loaded M-16 in her hands, firing prone, toward the KGB position, kneecapping a man, dropping him, catching another man in the groin, then again in the chest — a three-round coup de grace.

She kept firing, glancing to her right — Rourke was climbing the packing crates, gunfire hammering into the wall on both sides of him, cratering the concrete with blistering pockmarks, thudding into the crates beneath his feet and legs.

She burned out the magazine in the M-16, snatching up the third rifle, firing three-round bursts again, into the KGB position, headshooting an enlisted man as he made to fire his AKM toward Rourke.

Two more of the KGB unit rushed through the blown-apart doors — one man carried what she recognized as the 7.62mm PK General Purpose Machine Gun. It fired the Type 54R cartridge, and although the same caliber as standard Soviet service weapons, and utilizing the Kalishnikov rotating bolt, the cartridge was vastly more powerful, and from the size of the field green box beneath the receiver, she realized it carried either a two-hundred- or two-hundred-fifty-round link belt.

She fired her M-16 toward the two-man machine gun crew, dropping the gunner's assistant with a long ragged burst to the abdomen, but the machinegunner making it to cover.

"John! Machine gun!" She swapped magazines for all three rifles as she shouted to him.

He was lighting the fuse with the glowing tip of his cigar—she could see him, as if in freeze frame.

And then the machine gun opened up, the noise deafening as the reports echoed and reechoed in the confines of the abandoned machine shop, her heart stopping as the packing crates were shot out from under him and Rourke tumbled to the floor.

"Bastards!" She shrieked the word at the top of her voice, one M-16 slung under her right arm now as she stood, the other two M-16s—one in each hand—firing as she ran from cover, toward Rourke.

The machine gun was chewing into the wall behind her, chewing into the concrete flooring beneath her as she kept firing.

She heard a shout over the din of gunfire. "I'm all right!"

And then semiautomatic assault rifle fire—without looking, she knew Rourke was alive.

She kept firing, crossing the floor of the machine shop, the hammering of the PK's almost continuous fire maddening.

One M-16 was out, and then the second. Natalia let both weapons drop on their slings, swinging forward the third assault rifle, firing with it.

She was beside Rourke now, Rourke's CAR-15 spitting, then suddenly still.

There was a blur of motion and then the booming of his twin Detonics pistols.

"Run with me!"

She swallowed hard, moving—she would 'run with' him forever if he chose it.

Chapter Thirty-eight

Both Detonics pistols were empty as they reached the tunnel mouth, Rourke shoving Natalia ahead of him, then jumping after her, hitting the dirt surface of the tunnel floor hard, on knees and elbows crawling inside as the ground around him rippled with the plowing effect of the machine gun bursts.

He looked up at Natalia—she was changing sticks for all three M-16s. As he worked down the slide stop, ramming both Detonics pistols into his belt, empty, taking one of the M-16s from her, he rasped, breathless—"That fuse is lit—maybe a minute—" he sank forward, breathing hard.

"I know—run like hell," she laughed.

He looked at her, felt himself grin. "You got it."

And she was up, stooped over, but running, Rourke firing a burst from the M-16 through the tunnel mouth then running.

The heavy thudding of machine gun fire and the lighter reports of the AKMs was an echo behind them, now the echo diminishing.

But the Soviets would be following if they

hadn't noticed the fuse and shooting down the straight line of the tunnel, and he and Natalia would be slaughtered.

If they had noticed the fuse. . . .

He heard the gunfire, louder than it should have been, shoving Natalia down ahead of him, throwing his body over hers as bullets tore into the dirt and rock walls of the small tunnel, cut waves and ripples across the dirt of the tunnel floor.

Then he heard, feeling it almost before the actual noise reached his ears, burrowing his body even more across hers, his chest over her head, Rourke's hands going to his ears.

The tunnel floor trembled, shook—seemed to be twisting under them.

The concussion dying, Rourke pushed himself up, dragging Natalia to her feet, shoving her ahead.

He looked back once—a wall of flames behind him.

They were safe, at least until they reached the end of the tunnel and came out through the mouth of the small cave—at least until then.

And the KGB unit behind them—unless some had run for safety through the blown-out steel doors, they would all be dead. Where the dynamite had been situated, it would have torn the machinery to bits, then propelled it in a wave of shrapnel that would have destroyed anyone in its path.

He swallowed hard—but kept running.

Chapter Thirty-nine

The Womb had been reformed now, to suit the needs of Rozhdestvenskiy's orders — and his plans. It was no longer recognizable as NORAD Headquarters.

What had once been offices had been converted into a huge laboratory, and Rozhdestvenskiy, the conversion complete, did not this time supervise or observe from behind glass. He stood in the laboratory.

He watched the bluish glow of the almost luminescent gas that filled one of the twelve American chambers he had found.

He turned to Professor Zlovski, saying, "How long before we will know, doctor?"

"You must realize, comrade colonel — we can never know with full certainty until the actual event takes place. But the serum seems to have produced the desired effect. Yet, certain of the types of serum with which Soviet scientists experimented initially at least seemed to have the desired effect as well. It was not until the period of the experiment was concluded that we realized the serum had failed in its purpose in one aspect or another."

"So there is no certainty?"

"According to the data you have provided, comrade, it would seem that scientists both inside and outside the NASA establishment worked with the serum and that the desired results were achieved. And I do not doubt the validity of these reports and the sincerity of the research, but you must appreciate something—" and Zlovski, gray-haired, stroked his small, gray-black spade beard, his dark eyes staring past Rozhdestvenskiy, then taking on a peculiar light as he walked away, toward the nearest of the chambers, the one that had been activated. "An example, comrade colonel. Do you smoke—cigarettes? You do, I believe?"

"Yes—I smoke cigarettes—"

"That is excellent—not for your health, certainly, but for the sake of understanding my example—and this will illustrate the scientific dilemma in which we find ourselves. Now—at the earliest stages of research to discover a link between cigarette smoking and certain diseases. You can appreciate a critical factor—time. If prolonged smoking—say for a period of twenty years—is needed to produce symptoms in some or many cases, what is a scientist to do? We have no time machines, we have no way of bending time to our will. So, the process of cigarette smoking in laboratory animals was accelerated, to approximate the effect of time. With our experiment," and he stroked the top of the blue glowing chamber, "there was not even the possibility of acceleration. We are at the mercy of real time here—and there is no way to give positive results that will ease your mind, comrade, until the actual experiment has been performed. So, we either won't know for five hundred years, approximately, or, on the other hand," and his dark eyes gleamed, their corners crinkling with something Rozhdestvenskiy could only interpret as possible laughter, "we will never know."

Rozhdestvenskiy studied the glowing chamber, the swirling gases contained inside. "And what of the volunteer—when shall we know something?"

"The longer we can wait, the greater fraction of experimental validity we shall have—I can terminate the experiment now, after only a few hours. I can wait for days—the results might well be a bit more meaningful after a few days' duration than only a few hours. He is a volunteer, knew what he was volunteering to do."

"Regardless of the outcome, he shall receive decoration as a hero of the Soviet Union."

And it was laughter this time—Rozhdestvenskiy could not mistake it as he watched Professor Zlovski. "I have serious doubts, comrade colonel, whether the receipt of such an honor will impress our volunteer greatly, if at all, should the experiment prove to be unsuccessful. But do not despair—for I understand in discussions with some of my colleagues in the scientific establishment here that in the event of failure, The Womb can be hermetically sealed—"

"It will be, at any event," Rozhdestvenskiy interrupted, realizing his palms were sweating—nervousness.

"Quite—and with the hydroponic gardens that have been planted, oxygen/carbon-dioxide interchange would be of sufficient volume. So, we shall endure regardless."

"To live like moles?" Rozhdestvenskiy asked rhetorically, turning away from Zlovski, lighting a cigarette. Cigarette smoking was forbidden in the laboratory—it was why he lit it. "To live less than human existences? What does it matter to be masters of a lifeless world? Hmm? To never see the sun?"

"But comrade colonel—there are other avenues of endeavor besides the acquisition of power—are there not?"

"Yes," and Rozhdestvenskiy turned to face Zlovski. "The preservation of power."

He dropped his cigarette to the laboratory floor, heeling it out on the tiles there.

All he could hear as he walked away was the clicking of his heels and the faint mechanical hum of the chamber.

If he had not denounced all belief in God, he would have prayed then for the experiment to succeed.

Chapter Forty

Rourke had been there before—he had lectured there once to more than a hundred police officers. Before The Night of The War it had been a public shooting range and gunshop, before that a skating rink. The sign had fallen, was gone—but he knew the place anyway. Waukegan Outdoor Sportsman.

He stopped at the rear metal door, Emily tapping out some sort of code as she knocked.

A peephole had been cut in the steel door, and Rourke saw a tiny shaft of light in the gathering darkness—it was near sunset—when the peephole opened.

And then the peephole closed, the sound of metal scraping against metal, perhaps a security bar being lifted, and the door opened.

Emily stepped through, Rourke going ahead of Natalia, following Emily and, as he glanced back quickly, Dumbrowski and two other men following after.

There were no lights, and in the darkness—gray, indefinite, he could hear the door being closed behind them. A curtain—black, heavy, was ripped back and beyond the curtain burned dim ceiling lights. In a far corner of what had apparently been a shipping area, he heard the hum of a generator. He could smell its fumes.

It was cold in the building, and he followed Emily past new faces, eyes staring at them—Rourke tried to smile. No one smiled back. As they walked, Rourke rasped under his breath to Natalia, falling in beside her as he slowed his pace, "Let me do the talking—please."

She looked at him, her blue eyes flashing—but she nodded, blinking her eyes closed for an instant as she did—it was like the light flickered out of the world when she closed them, he thought.

They passed through a storage area—there were weapons of all descriptions on tables and on the floors, most disassembled. Reloading presses were in operation, children attending them. As they walked on, two men appeared, one older, one young, both men going to one of the tables, commencing to work on one of the firearms there.

They passed into what Rourke remembered had been the sales floor of the retail store—it was now a hospital, apparently.

"How many people have been treated here?" Rourke asked Emily Bronkiewicz.

"Maybe a thousand since The Night of The War. We have some real doctors, and we have a lot of volunteers. Some of the tougher cases— well, they can't do anything for them. My husband—he was one of 'em," and her eyes flickered to Natalia, but this time the woman smiled.

173

The woman started up a flight of stairs, Rourke going ahead of Natalia again, following Emily. As they climbed the stairs, he could overlook the vast square footage — he estimated more than a hundred beds in use, crammed together with barely enough room to walk between. And few of them were beds — most were mats, some packing boxes.

The woman turned down a small corridor, past open office doors, men inside the offices, sometimes a face looking up, then quickly turning away.

She stopped at the last office, the door open.

A man perhaps Rourke's own age, perhaps a little younger, looked up from a paper-littered desk. His face lit up with a smile beneath his close-cropped, light-colored, curly hair.

His eyes seemed to radiate a good humor Rourke had seen in none of the other men or women of the local Resistance. And Rourke remembered the man. "It's Maus, isn't it?"

"Tom Maus," the man said, rising from his seat, extending his right hand, Rourke took it. "And you're — John Rourke, right? The M.D. who taught survivalism and weapons training — I remember the presentation you gave."

"That's right," Rourke nodded. He watched Maus's eyes as they took in Natalia.

"And you, miss — I know your face, too — it's Major Tiemerovna of the KGB — mistress or maybe the wife of Karamatsov before he was killed."

"Wife," Rourke heard Natalia answer — lifelessly.

"I guess that's kind of a negative way of starting a conversation, though, isn't it — I didn't mean anything by it. Before the war I used to think I was busy — Reserves, running the shop here, the wholesaling business — hell, I wish I had that much free time now. I get a little testy when I'm tired. Why don't we all sit down."

Rourke looked at Natalia — her face seemed to show that she had relaxed — if only a little.

"Emily," Maus said. "Good to see you're still alive —" and Maus grinned as he looked at Rourke. "Her husband was one of the best field people I had — and she's better. But I still miss him. I'd offer you coffee but I don't like poisoning people — and the pop machine never worked that well before The Night of The War and anyway we ran out of pop."

"We're fine," Rourke nodded.

He noticed Maus looking at Natalia, and then Maus spoke. "I know a lot about you, major — heard through U.S. II all the scuttlebutt about what you did in Florida during the quakes. And I also know through our sources — we have some spies who take a lot of risks and sometimes get us pretty good information — so I know that the KGB has you on some kind of hit list — wants you dead. Why, I don't know. So," Maus looked at Rourke then. "Like I said — nothin' I like better than renewing old acquaintances, but I've got a field hospital to run, a weapons repair shop, a reloading operation —"

"What's where the range used to be?" Rourke asked him, interrupting. "More beds?"

"No—we can't accommodate the people we have out on the floor down there—no. Since it's soundproofed, we use it as a training area, a testing area for the weapons we repair—everything it needs to be used for—and a few other things besides. But like I said, if I had twelve hands, I still wouldn't have a thumb to twiddle—so why are you both here? Something for U.S. II or what?"

Rourke shrugged, saying to Natalia as he looked at her, "You explain it—all of it. We can trust this man."

Natalia's eyes—they seemed to look into his soul, Rourke thought, but then she turned to look at Maus. "My uncle is General Varakov, the supreme commander—"

"I sort of figured he was some kind of relative of yours—go ahead."

And, gradually, she told Tom Maus everything.

Chapter Forty-one

The hospital that occupied the sales floor of Waukegan Outdoor Sportsman, and had almost since The Night of The War, was known to the Soviet authorities — General Varakov periodically sent teams of Soviet doctors into the hospital to help however they could, and what medical supplies — meager — could be spared were sent as well. The plans were simple — when Soviet patrols were in the area, or an inspection was due, or the medical team was to be sent, the beds were spread out into the range area and the weapons and reloading equipment hidden in an underground area left from an old storm drain.

It was risky business, Rourke knew, the timing critical, a gap in information potentially fatal. If the underground storage area were discovered, or the equipment not gotten away in time, or the beds not spread out in time — a firing squad.

Even General Varakov would have no other choice, Rourke realized.

And Maus was risking his entire operation now — he had provided Rourke with medical credentials, and Natalia as well, medical credentials that would serve as travel permits. And he had loaned them an automobile, the kind of loan Rourke knew Maus had realized would never be returned.

Rourke's false identity listed him as "Peter Masters," a dead Resistance fighter in reality, but on paper a hospital volunteer with little medical background. To have listed Rourke as an M.D. would have been suicidal—all medical doctors were registered with Soviet headquarters, Maus had said, and Natalia confirmed it. Natalia was listed as "Mary Ann Klein," another volunteer.

The travel request—Maus had signed it as administrator of the de facto hospital—indicated they were en route to the Soviet Mobile Surgical Unit stationed at Soldier's Field Stadium to request a fresh supply of hypodermic syringes. Maus had used the system before, for the actual procurement of medical supplies, and to cover covert operations of his Resistance command.

Somewhat the statistician, Maus had predicted odds of three to one that the travel documents would get them through, at least as far as the stadium.

And medical emergency was the only even remotely justified purpose for nighttime travel.

They had passed the Belvedere Road checkpoint leaving Waukegan—no difficulties there, Rourke driving. They had passed two checkpoints along what had been the Illinois Tollway, no difficulties either. The checkpoint on the Edens Expressway had been something both Rourke and Natalia had

178

sweated, Rourke watching her eyes as the Soviet officer in charge of the checkpoint had been summoned to examine their travel documents. But they had been allowed to move on their way.

Their risk was doubly great — concealed in a hidden compartment of what had been the gas tank, accessible by going through the firewall from the inside or outside of the trunk of the vintage Ford LTD, were their weapons and gear. Should these be discovered, it would mean instant death. To compensate for the Ford's reduced gasoline tank, an auxiliary tank had been rigged partially under the rear seat — Rourke wouldn't have wanted to have been in the car in case of high-speed impact, he had decided.

The checkpoint leaving the Edens and entering the Kennedy Expressway had been almost too simple.

They had proceeded.

There was a long line of military vehicles ahead of them as they came within the boundaries of what had been the Chicago Loop, the downtown shopping and business district. As they drove, Natalia had described to him what it had been like there after The Night of The War — wild dog packs which had come in from outside the neutron bomb area, roving gangs of thugs who lived like rats beneath the once great department stores and in the abandoned subway tunnels. Soviet troops would chase after them, but for the most part — this urban equivalent of Brigands would vanish before the soldiers could close with them. The urban Brigands were armed with everything from stolen

Soviet assault rifles to clubs, some of the bands re-sorting to the behavior of beasts, Natalia had told him.

She had not amplified.

They sat now, the engine running, the LTD advancing a car length at a time toward the checkpoint. Natalia spoke. "This checkpoint is staffed by KGB—and the army too, but the main staffing is a KGB unit."

"You think they'll recognize you." It was a statement, not a question.

"I could only do so much—putting my hair up under this," and Rourke looked at her as she gestured to the scarf covering her hair, "and these glasses—" Maus had given her the glasses of a dead woman who had expired at the hospital—the woman had been farsighted and Natalia had had trouble walking when she wore them to the car. It was the reason Rourke drove and had not shared the long run with her. "And your face—it is known to many of the KGB."

Rourke wore a hat borrowed from the supply of old clothing kept at the Resistance headquarters, an old fedora, gray, stained. It matched the overcoat he wore.

"What are you getting at?" Rourke finally asked her, beginning to worry the car might overheat—the engine was already stalling a little as he advanced another car length toward the checkpoint. He had spent a good amount of time in Chicago before The Night of The War, learned the streets. The checkpoint was at the near side of the tunnel near Hubbard Street.

"I don't know—but maybe we should make a break for it."

Rourke looked around them, not answering Natalia's question. A troop truck flanked them on the left, an M-72 motorcycle/sidecar combination on the right. "Where do you suggest we go—up?"

"I wish that we could," she answered, lighting a cigarette—she was nervous, he realized.

Perhaps it was, in part, just the very fact of being in Chicago, Soviet headquarters so near. KGB everywhere. He said to her, "If they spot us at all, it won't be until we reach the checkpoint gate—and if it happens there, we can make a break for it then. If we do, ditch those glasses so you can see and rip out the back seat so you can get to that panel inside the truck and get at the weapons." And then Rourke smiled, looking at her with the scarf covering her hair and the tattered raincoat that all but obscured her figure. "And if we do make a break for it, get rid of that scarf and that coat—if we wind up dying, I wanna at least have something pretty to look at while I can still look."

She smiled, then very quickly, as if someone might see, leaned across the front seat, across the space separating them, kissing him on the cheek.

Chapter Forty-two

The checkpoint was at what, before the war, had sometimes been called Hubbard's Cave.

Rourke eased the old LTD to the gate that blocked his lane.

A green-shouldered, bearded KGB noncom approached the car, Rourke rolling down his window. In poor English, the man stated, "Civilian traffic is expressly forbidden after sunset—"

Rourke smiled his warmest smile, interrupting the man, "Except for medical emergencies, right?" Rourke passed the man his papers.

The man unfolded the letter Maus had signed as director of the civilian hospital in the con verted gunshop and shooting range. "Hippoder mineed—"

"Hypodermic needles," Rourke corrected. "Can't give shots with dirty needles—hepatitis, stuff like that."

The man unfolded Rourke's identity papers, looking at Rourke—apparently trying to match the physical description with the face—it should match, Rourke thought. The forger had been looking at his face while counterfeiting the identity papers.

"And her?" the man said.

Rourke turned to look at Natalia — fear was written across her face so that a blind man could have almost known it, he thought. She handed him her papers from the battered brown vinyl purse that had come with the old raincoat.

Rourke passed them over to the KGB noncom. "Here you go," he smiled. "Say look — we got a lot of sick people up there — need those needles. The hypodermics."

There had been one other risk for Maus — that if they were discovered and traced back to the hospital, there would be a raid, and the Resistance headquarters destroyed. Rourke considered that now as he watched the man, studying Natalia's forged documents, peering into the car, a flashlight in his right hand, the beam high, trained on Natalia's face.

Rourke made a decision.

"Major Tiemerovna!"

As the man gasped her name, Rourke wrenched the LTD's door handle — he had prepared to do it, and he slammed the door hard outward, against the abdomen of the KGB noncom, hammering the man back.

Rourke reached out of the car, stepping half out of the driver's seat, his left hand grabbing for the military flap holster on the man's belt, his right grabbing for the papers — he had them all.

The pistol — Rourke stuffed the papers into the pocket of his borrowed overcoat, worked the slide of the pistol in case a round hadn't been chambered — none had. He pointed the pistol at the KGB noncom's face — the mouth was open to shout for aid. Rourke emptied the pistol into the man's mouth, then threw it down to the pavement, the door not closed as he stomped the accelerator, the door slamming as it whacked against the side of the barricade, Rourke throwing the hat out the window as he ducked, shouting to Natalia, "Down!"

Gunfire shattered the rear window, bullet holes spiderwebbing the windshield in front of him, the accelerator already flat to the floor, the speedometer needle passing fifty and climbing fast — he'd always liked eight cylinder Fords.

Chapter Forty-three

"I'm going for the guns," Natalia shouted, Rourke shooting a glance toward her—he smiled. She had ripped away the scarf that had covered her hair, shaking her head now, freeing her hair like a wild animal, something untamed, might shake itself at the first taste of freedom. She smiled at him—they both understood what she had done. Death might be imminent.

Behind them, motorcycle/sidecar combinations were rolling, headlights bouncing as the vehicles accelerated, their noise loud in the cold night air through Rourke's open window.

"Before you get the guns—burn these—" and Rourke fisted the papers in his overcoat pocket, making sure he had them all, handing them across to Natalia.

"Right—" She bent to the floor as he looked at her, lighting them with her cigarette lighter—the papers were on fire.

He turned his attention to the road—an automobile—with Chicago Police markings obliterated by a red star. It was moving diagonally across the highway, cutting them off. He could hear Natalia stamping her feet — "Nothing but ashes."

"Now get us some guns — we got friends comin' up on the left."

Rourke started steering right, the police car cutting them off. Natalia — at the edge of his peripheral vision he could see her going over into the back seat to start getting the weapons.

The blue and white car was too close — Rourke cut the wheel hard left, shouting over the wind of the slipstream, "Hang on — collision!"

The right front fender — he could see it, hear it, feel it as it smashed against the right rear fender of the police car, the sounds of metal twisting, tearing, the bumper of the police car twisting up to where it was visible over the LTD's hood, the Ford straining, dragging at the police car, Rourke accelerating, another tearing sound, louder than before — the LTD shot ahead.

In the rearview mirror he could see the police car, making a high-speed reverse, flick turning, the twisted bumper breaking off, the blue light flashing from the roof. There was the rattle of assault rifle fire, Rourke shouting to Natalia, "AKMs — keep low!"

The rear windshield shattered out, Rourke swerving as more gunfire poured toward them, Rourke hearing it pinging against the body of the Ford. He cut sharp right, onto a ramp — he didn't know where he was heading, no time to look and Chicago streets and expressways not that recent a memory.

He fought the wheel, shouting, "Natalia—are you all right?"

The rear end of the Ford was fishtailing as he curved the entrance ramp at nearly fifty, sideswiping the guardrail, the Eisenhower Expressway opening up before him—the post office interchange coming up fast—they were passing the post office now, Rourke shouting again to Natalia as he picked up more blue lights in the rearview mirror.

"Natalia!"

"Yes—I'm all right—I almost have them!"

Rourke cut the wheel hard left, shouting, "Hang on!" a police car starting toward them going against the direction of the lanes—but there was no traffic, just abandoned cars flanking the expressway in both lanes on both shoulders. Rourke stomped the accelerator to the floor, shooting an intersection, into the Loop now, the police car on a collision course with them.

Gunfire—from behind him, the police car suddenly swerving, its windshield shattered, another shot, the police car accelerating, Rourke cutting a sharp right to miss it, in the rear view seeing Natalia, holding one of her revolvers, and the police car crashing into an underpass abutment behind them.

Rourke started to edge left, turning toward State Street. "It was made into a shopping mall—it could be cut off," Natalia shouted.

Rourke cut back right— "Back seat driver," taking the next left—Wabash.

Police cars—four abreast—were coming down

Wabash, against him, he cut left at Jackson Boulevard — heading against the flow of traffic had there been traffic — a one-way street, the signs half down but still visible.

"Just as well," he shouted to her — "High speed on Wabash with the elevated train platform — suicide." And he stomped the gas pedal, crossing State, Dearborn, heading west, the city empty, ghostly, one out of every ten or so street lights burning — Rourke guessed the Russians had gotten power restored at least to parts of the city. But the street lamps were mostly shot out or otherwise shattered, it seemed, as he sped under them.

Natalia was back beside him now — "The rest of our gear — it's in the back seat — here," and she handed him a pistol — one of the little Detonics stainless .45s — she knew what he liked, he thought. "Chamber's loaded, hammer down," she advised.

Rourke rammed the pistol into his belt, ripping open the overcoat buttons, swerving to avoid the body of a dead dog — and suddenly, behind him, there was a pack — the animals running after the car, the police cars two blocks back not frightening them off — Rourke swerved close to a curb to avoid a wrecked car in the middle of the street — he almost lost control of the Ford as a huge dog leapt out toward the car from the roof of an abandoned car — it was on the hood, snarling, foam dripping from its mouth — "Shoot it, for God's sake," Rourke shouted to Natalia.

He looked to his right — already she was leaning out the passenger side window, one of her revolvers in her right hand, the dog snapping at the windshield, somehow balancing itself on the hood.

There was a loud shot—felt in his right ear. The dog's head seemed to explode, the animal's body flopping to Rourke's left, blood and gray material that was brain splattering the windshield. The body slid from the hood of the car as Rourke swerved right.

He found the windshield wiper switch—only one wiper blade—in front of the driver's side. The other was bare metal. He punched the washer button on the wiper control switch—nothing— "Aww, shit," Rourke rasped—the blood and brain matter were smeared now like grease, all but obscuring the windshield—he kept the wiper blade going, hoping to at least scrape some of the mess away.

More police cars—closing from the streets he crossed, falling in, almost like a formation, behind those already in pursuit.

Wacker Drive—Rourke turned right, accelerating, police cars behind him now but still nothing ahead—the Civic Opera House—he had given a lecture there once, he recalled—police cars now blocking the street ahead of him.

He shouted to Natalia, "Did you ever block out underground Wacker Drive?"

"No—we couldn't leave workers down there— the Brigands—some of their bodies—they were eaten partially—arms cut off and legs—and our pathologists said they weren't dogs who had done it—people."

Rourke looked at her, sucked in his breath,

rasping, "Reach into my pocket and find me a cigar — soon as I do this," and Rourke cut the wheel hard left, half bouncing over a lip of concrete curb, turning sharp right, fishtailing, skidding, his lights making bizarre patterns as he drove into the velvet blackness of the underground.

Chapter Forty-four

In the darkness—total darkness except for the headlights and the few working dashboard lights—he could feel Natalia's right hand reach across him, searching his breast pocket for a cigar. "Lit?"

"Not with that auxiliary gas tank," he told her, swerving sharp left, nearly piling up in a divider, the car bouncing away from it as he avoided a pile of cement blocks in the middle of the road.

And suddenly the cavernlike underground drive was illuminated, an almost surreal blue wash of light, sirens loud in the distance behind him— more of the expropriated police squad cars. And there were single headlights too—motorcycles, he guessed.

Rourke stepped hard on the gas.

Beside him, the headlights of the police vehicles and the motorcycles growing fast now, Natalia had an M-16—she was leaning out of the passenger window— "Watch out when I run close to the tunnel walls!" He heard it, felt it—the pelting of hot brass against his bare skin, his hands, his neck, his right cheek.

A set of headlights behind them swerved maddeningly to the right, a blinding flash in the darkness, a bright orange wall of flame, but punching through the wall — one set of headlights, then another, and then a single headlight — a motorcycle. The sidecar visible in the light of the fire was aflame, a man shape moving in it, arms waving, arms like torches, then the single headlight seemed to jump skyward as Natalia's M-16 loosed a long, ragged burst, sidecar and motorcycle separating, crashing into opposite sides of the tunnel walls — flames. Two police cars, their Mars lights flashing blue in the darkness as Rourke took a sharp curving right, police cars and motorcycles coming fast from his right flank as he passed another entrance into Underground Wacker.

The entire tunnel was washed in the blue light of the flashers now as Rourke made the Ford accelerate, swerving the wheel left, right, left again, evading abandoned automobiles left everywhere in the narrow confines of the underground, dog packs running across his lights, yelping, snarling, some of the animals leaping upward as he passed them, fangs bared.

A massive animal — almost too large to be a dog, Rourke thought — it leaped from the hood of an abandoned car, Natalia screaming as he looked right, the dog half inside the vehicle, Rourke's right hand snatching at the Pachmayr gripped butt of the Detonics, his thumb jerking back the trigger.

He fired the pistol once, twice, a third time, point blank into the chest of the animal as it lunged for Natalia's throat.

His ears rang with the gunfire, but the animal still moved, a low roaring gunshot, partially muffled, the animal slumping as Natalia pushed close to Rourke—her face normally had a paleness to it, an almost unnatural whiteness—what men another time would have called alabaster. But her cheeks were flushed bright red now—and her eyes were larger-seeming than he thought human eyes could be.

"That—" she gasped.

"Did he break the skin—at all—" Rourke shouted, not looking at her, swerving to avoid an overturned green dumpster spilling out from the sidewalk backing the underground entrances to buildings and restaurants.

"No—thank God—there—I said it again," she laughed.

Rourke glanced at her, then back at the tunnel. It was coming into a sharp right—Rourke cut the wheel hard, shouting to her, "Push the dog out after I finish the turn."

He felt Natalia clinging to him as he cut the wheel all the way right, the Ford's rear end fishtailing, Rourke's hands moving over the wheel as he recovered fast, straightening out, the squealing of tires behind him, headlights dancing maddeningly along the tunnel walls in his rearview mirror.

He felt Natalia moving now— "Heavy," he heard her gasp, and he heard the car door opening, then after a moment slamming shut.

He looked across at her—one of the L-Frame Smiths was in her right hand still. It was her shot that had finished the dog, he realized.

The Detonics still in his right hand as he held the wheel, cocked and locked, Rourke hammered down on the accelerator. It was narrowing ahead, and pylons dotted the roadway, pylons that, under normal conditions at normal speeds would have made driving difficult.

Gunfire echoed from behind them—the police cars closing, and more of the motorcycles coming up in the rearview as well. The bullet hole spiderwebbed windshield, smeared with the blood and brain matter of the wild dog that had climbed onto the hood, the windshield wiper scraping screechingly across it—Rourke peered ahead.

Somehow he'd lost one of his headlights and the velvet darkness beyond the single yellowed beam was blacker still.

Chapter Forty-five

It was as though he was trying to thread a surgical needle, Rourke thought, sideswiping a pylon as he zigzagged his way through the underground. The police vehicles were closing. One of the motorcycles in the opposite lane now, coming up faster than he could risk driving the LTD through the obstacle course. Besides the normal obstacles of the pylons, abandoned cars littered the roadside on the building side to his right and the opening to the Chicago River on his left. Trash dumpsters, garbage cans, the bones and half-devoured bodies of dead animals — and men — were sprinkled about the road surface like discarded toys.

"Watch out for the seat there — if that dog left any fleas behind they could be carrying God knows what on them. This is contagion city — "

"We have sprayed — "

"Even the neutron bombing wouldn't have done any good — these dogs couldn't have survived that — like you said, they came from outside the city bringing fleas and ticks with them — stay as clear as you can of that part of the seat — and don't touch your hands to your face or hair—I've got stuff in my pack that you can use to clean up."

"That motorcycle—it's coming up fast—the man in the sidecar—I think that's an RPK light machine gun he's got."

"Wonderful," Rourke rasped, glancing into his side-view mirror—the M-72 motorcycle/sidecar combination was a car's length behind him now—the man in the sidecar manipulating a weapon, getting ready to fire.

Rourke still grasped the Detonics .45 in his right fist. He rammed it out the open driver's side window and fired it out, three rounds, the pistol rocking hard in his hand, his wrist bent to aim the gun.

The motorcycle swerved, but wasn't stopped.

Rourke gained a single car length.

His right thumb worked the slide stop down, the slide running forward as he rammed the pistol into his belt, empty.

Ahead of him, the tunnel seemed to be opening—it would be the underground section of the Michigan Avenue bridge, he realized. He started cranking the wheel left, machine gun fire hammering into the driver's side door, the rear end of the LTD fishtailing right, Natalia shouting, "Don't move your head—" The muzzle of an M-16 was shoved in front of him, between his face and the cracked and smeared windshield, fire from the muzzle, Rourke craning his head back, glancing left—Natalia had knocked out the LMG on the motorcycle/sidecar combination, the motorcycle itself spinning out, crashing against a pylon.

He started recovering the wheel, accelerating as

he straightened out into the underground level of the bridge.

There was a humming sound, rubber tires over metal gratings, bouncing and thudding sensation as the Ford shot ahead.

In the rearview, he could see three police cars and two more motorcycles. He kept accelerating. Natalia screamed, "The bridge—there's a nine-foot section out at the far side—John!"

"Shit!"

Rourke hammered the accelerator to the floor—his eyes searching through the darkness to find the hole in the bridge—and ahead, a darker patch than the darkness of the roadway, to his right a high curb. Rourke cut the wheel hard right, then left, the LTD skidding, the rear end swaying, the steering all but gone as he accelerated, the rear end impacting the curb as he turned away, two of the police cars coming at him, skidding as they tried to brake—one swerved left—crashing into the bridge supports, the second rocketed past him, Rourke nearly crashing the LTD into it broadside, the headlights there one instant then gone the next. As he fought the wheel, a fountain of river water sprayed up, spraying the LTD for an instant, but then the wheel was all the way left, Rourke heading away from the hole in the bridge, the third squad car and the two motorcycle units coming dead on, the biker units flanking the police car, consuming the entire width of the bridge.

"Gimme a gun!"

He reached out his right hand, feeling the memory-grooved smooth Goncalo Alves stocks of one of her matched L-Frames coming into his palm. He switched the revolver to his left hand, ramming the hand out the driver's side window, his right fist locked at the top of the wheel. Natalia was rolling over into the back seat, an M-16 in her hands as he glanced at her.

The LMG on the M-72 combination to Rourke's left was firing, and then the LMG from the sidecar to his right — AKM fire streamed toward them from the passenger side of the solitary police car.

Natalia's assault rifle fire — it reverberated from the back seat, the sounds of empty brass pinging against the frame of the open window, Rourke's left fist clenched tight on the L-Frame, his right rock-steady on the wheel to give as sure a firing platform as possible — he was aiming for the police car — aiming the LTD straight at it.

The L-Frame in his left fist — he pumped the trigger, double-actioning two rounds toward the M-72 combination to his left. He fired twice more — the motorcyclist threw his hands out from his handlebars, slumping back, the machine gunner in the sidecar reaching for the bike's controls suddenly, then jumping clear, Rourke shouting to Natalia, "Watch out!"

He cut the wheel hard left, evading the motorcycle, the combination crashing into one of the bridge supports to his left, Natalia's M-16 still firing as they passed the squad car, AKM fire ripping across the driver's compartment, his windshield shooting out, the rearview mirror gone, the speedometer, the gas gauge — all of it shattered, a ribbon of bullet holes across the dashboard.

Rourke accelerated — past the underground tunnel running parallel to the river, into what looked like a box canyon of building walls ahead of him, shouting, "Natalia? You all right?"

"So far," he heard her shout back to him.

"Hold on — flick turn," and Rourke dropped the L-Frame to his lap, holding it between his legs, cutting the wheel sharply to the left as he stomped the emergency brake, locking the rear wheels, then popping the brake as the car rotated a full one hundred eighty degrees, accelerating as he fought the wheel, then flooring it as he aimed toward the last of the motorcycle combinations, the police car turning behind it.

Rourke could see the face of the machine gunner in the sidecar — and then it was gone, Rourke rocking the wheel hard left, into the combination, then hard right and away, hearing a scream die on the slipstream, blood splattering the few shards of glass left in the windshield, Natalia's M-16 firing again toward the oncoming police car, the AKM firing from the passenger window, Rourke's left hand finding the L-Frame-two shots left.

He stabbed the revolver through the open windshield ahead of his face, his right fist white-knuckled on the top of the Ford's steering wheel.

He fired once, then once again, the windshield of the advancing police car shattering, Natalia's M-16 fire increasing its rate — she had to have shot through a full magazine in seconds, he realized, but the gunfire continued, sparks coming from the police car's hood, a stricken face suddenly visible behind the wheel as Rourke swerved the Ford to avoid a head-on collision, the LTD's single head-light catching the face in freeze frame.

A bridge support—Rourke fought at the wheel—there was no response—he stomped the brakes, the rear end of the Ford fishtailing right, Rourke shouting to Natalia, "Hit the floor! Hit the floor!"

He held the wheel as long as he dared, then threw himself down to the floor over the hump, his body shuddering as he felt the impact, heard the twisting and tearing of steel.

Smoke—he smelled gasoline fumes.

His back hurt a little—he pushed himself up.

Natalia was already up— "I've got the packs and everything—all the gear—"

"Out of the car and—"

"Run like hell," she almost laughed, Rourke seeing her streak through the rear driver's side door and out, Rourke, the L-Frame in his belt now beside the Detonics, half rolling, half falling from the driver's side of the front seat.

On his feet, his hands grabbing at the lapels of the overcoat, ripping it free of his body as he ran—

He felt it—like a giant's breath blowing at him, throwing himself to the road surface, shouting to Natalia, "Down!"

He shielded his face and head, the roar of the explosion—the gas tank—deafening as it echoed from the steel of the bridge above him and below.

The bridge shook—Rourke's mind raced—if it collapsed it collapsed—

The shaking stopped, and John Rourke looked up, the crackle of the fire from the LTD that had served them so well all that he could hear over the ringing in his ears.

And Natalia was beside him — holding him.

Chapter Forty-six

The Low Alpine Systems Loco pack on his shoulders, his guns back where they belonged, Natalia's hands cleaned and clothing checked for fleas or ticks, they walked through the underground now — gray light in patches only through gratings leading up to the street. If he remembered his Chicago streets well enough, they had a short distance only to go until coming up on Lake Street between Michigan and Wabash.

But Rourke stopped — hearing sounds.

"Dogs?" Natalia whispered hoarsely.

The growling sounds increased.

"Not dogs — " and he looked back — shadowy figures moved in the edge of light from the still burning Ford — it looked like one of the figures carried a human limb. "Imagination," he whispered, more to himself than Natalia.

He risked no flashlight, moving ahead.

The growling sounds again.

Natalia close beside him, Rourke hearing the telltale click of the selector on her M-16.

Rourke spoke into the darkness. "If you're hungry—there are dead men all over the bridge behind us. We're heavily armed and in too much of a hurry to be gentle—let us pass and we'll leave you unharmed."

The growling sounds again.

"John!"

And then Rourke heard a voice, nearly human sounding, "A woman—"

Rourke turned toward the origin of the voice in the darkness. "Let it be—or you're meat, too."

"Woman!" It was another voice now. "Woman!" Still another. And then, like chanting, "Woman—woman—woman—woman—woman—" and with each repetition, the chanting grew louder, voices adding to it.

"I guess they aren't just hungry," Rourke observed, Natalia close beside him—very close.

"Woman—woman—woman—woman—woman—woman—woman—"

Rourke raised the Kel-Lite in his left fist, high over his head, snapping the switch—eyes glowed in the beam of the flashlight, more eyes than he could count, human eyes, but strangely not human. To Natalia, Rourke rasped, "Stay close to me—we're backing out of here—I am—you walk forward—we stay back to back—shoot anything that moves—when we reach what looks like a ramp, take the left and start up it."

"I'm afraid," she whispered.

"Me too," he told the darkness where she was.

He felt her move, felt her rear end pressing against him, as they stood back to back.

"Start walking," Rourke almost whispered.

"Woman — woman — woman — woman — woman — woman — woman — "

Rourke pumped the M-16's trigger once, a
short, two-round burst — "Automatic weapons —
you don't stand a chance — "

There was a moan in the darkness.

The chanting never stopped, "Woman — woman — woman — woman — woman — "

"On my left, your right," he heard Natalia whisper —

Rourke shot a glance right — movement in the
shadows, and now, above the chanting he could
hear the shuffling of feet.

Rourke killed the light, ramming it into his belt
as he swung the muzzle of the M-16 left to right
and back left, pumping the trigger, fighting the
muzzle climb, blowing half a magazine into the
darkness — "Run for it — fast!"

Rourke reached into the darkness — he had Natalia's shoulder — he knotted his fist into her pack-
strap, running beside her on her right, firing into
the darkness, Natalia firing now, but louder than
the firing, the chanting, "Woman!"

They ran toward the brighter grayness that
would be the exit up to Lake Street, and as the
light grew, Rourke's fear grew — flanking them
and behind them were men, dozens, more than
that — clubs, machetes, axes in their hands, trash
can lids held like shields, men in rags, filth seeming to drip from them, their flesh as gray as the
light, and as one man can — Rourke almost retched
and he heard Natalia gasp, almost scream — the

man chewed a still living rat, the rat between the man's teeth.

The M-16 was empty, Rourke taking no time to reload or shift to another firearm — almost dragging Natalia with him as they ran.

The ramp up to Lake Street — they turned into it, the darkness of the outside world bright by comparison, running up the steep incline, rocks and bottles pelting the street beside them, windows in the buildings on both sides smashing as faces appeared there — the chanting — "Woman!"

He didn't know whether they wanted to consume her flesh, rape her, or do both simultaneously — they were insane.

An automobile, wrecked, and then another — they were being pushed into the mouth of the street, blocking them into the ramp — flame — one automobile, then the second — afire now, the howling chants from behind them louder, from both sides of them as more rocks and bottles hammered down toward them.

Rourke rammed a fresh magazine into the M-16, shouting to Natalia over the screaming and wailing din — "Your purse — protect your face with it — I'll take care of the shooting!"

He looked at her once — terror in her eyes — and she obeyed, her M-16s swinging on their slings, her black shoulder bag up over her head as she bent into the run.

Rourke fired his M-16 to right and left, into the windows of the flanking buildings, to stop the fusillade of rocks and bottles and bricks and chunks of paving stones.

Natalia stumbled — he could see her — but she kept running as a brick hammered against her, bouncing from her backpack — a bottle thudded against Rourke's face, his right cheek taking the impact — he lost his cigar butt.

The bottle shattered at his feet as he ran.

The M-16 was empty and he let it fall to his right side on its sling, Rourke's hands going under his coat, finding both Detonics pistols, firing one from each hand simultaneously as they raced for the burning cars blocking their path.

Men — if men they still were — were beside the burning cars, hurtling rocks and bottles.

Rourke killed as many as he could until the pistols came up empty.

Actions still open, he rammed both pistols into his belt, taking the Colt Government model, working the slide, jacking a round into the chamber, firing as he ran.

Natalia's purse was back at her side — her revolvers in her hands, belching fire, thundering as she ran toward the burning automobiles.

The .45 was empty, Rourke rammed it into his belt — crowded with the twin Detonics pistols already there. The Python. He drew with his right hand, shifting to his left. He found the two-inch Lawman in the Thad Rybka holster in the small of his back, the Lawman in his right fist — both revolvers firing.

Natalia's revolvers were empty, he realized — the revolvers gone, the second M-16 in her hands, spitting fire.

Rourke's revolvers emptied as they reached the

206

burning cars, few of the men there now, some running, most dead.

Rourke holstered his revolvers, his hands going out to Natalia—there was a section of the barrier already burned out— "Don't touch the metal—jump when I get you up there—hurry!"

Rourke had her up in his arms, her feet on the blackened hood of a wrecked Cadillac, and she ran one step, jumped—he heard her scream.

"Shit!" Rourke snarled—he ran back from beside the cars, the CAR-15 his only loaded gun now as he threw himself into a dead run for the Cadillac's hood—he jumped, nearly slipping, the metal hot through the soles of his combat boots as he jumped clear, Natalia on the other side of the barricade, the silenced Walther in her right fist, the slide back—the gun was empty. She crashed it down across the face of a rag-clad man grabbing for her—the man fell in a heap at her feet.

More men coming for her—the chanting loud now from both sides of the burning barrier, Rourke's CAR-15 firing from his right hand—the trigger pumping, bodies falling as he closed toward her, killing his way to her.

The Bali-Song knife was in her right hand, the fancy Gerber-Mk II in her left, men lunging for her—not attacking, but wanting to grab her, he realized—to touch her.

The knives flashed, like a well-practiced martial arts Cata, ears, hands, noses, and fingers falling to the sidewalk as she fought.

Rourke's CAR-15 empty, he worked the telescoped stock like a club, a horizontal butt stroke to the face of one of the men, a forward butt stroke to another, using the flash deflector like a bayonet now, knifing down, slashing across the neck and face of another.

The big Gerber from his belt — it was in his right hand now as he let the rifle fall on its sling — he hacked with it, like a short sword, slicing across faces and necks, stabbing out with it — the attackers were endless.

Natalia screamed to him — "John!"

She had fallen — at least six men lunging for her.

Chapter Forty-seven

Rourke threw himself toward the men, his left foot snaking out as he half wheeled right, the sole of his combat boot impacting a jaw in a double Tae-Kwon-Do kick, his right hand still holding the knife stabbing into a second man.

He finished the turn, his right foot in a short, jabbing kick to the groin of a third man, Rourke's knife blade hacking upward, catching the nose and cheek — ripping flesh as blood sprayed.

He wheeled again, his right elbow hammering back as a man came from his right flank, the point of his elbow contacting bone — Rourke hissing with the pain — but feeling bone crunch, not his own.

He sidestepped, knifing another man in the throat, as a swordsman would make his lunge, Rourke's left hand stabbing outward, the middle knuckle impacting beneath the nose of another man, breaking it, bringing the bone up and puncturing the ethmoid bone — the nose driven up into the brain, the man's eyes rolled as he fell back dead.

The knife in his right hand flashed again — slick and red and wet with blood now — chopping through the neck of another man.

And Rourke was beside Natalia, Natalia up, her knives working, cutting and stabbing.

Rourke stabbed a man with a club — in the center of the adam's apple — he withdrew the knife, finding a spare magazine for one of the .45s — one of the eight-round extension magazines. He buttoned out the magazine in the big Colt, losing it on the sidewalk, ramming the fresh magazine home, working down the slide stop — he fired point blank, shooting away the face of one of the attackers, the Gerber in his left fist now slashing outward — another man down.

He fired the .45 a second time and a third, two men going down — "An opening, John!"

It was Natalia — he looked to his right, pumping the trigger of the Colt again — another man down — an opening in the wall of attackers, Natalia running for it, Rourke almost shoving her ahead.

He fired the .45 into the gaping mouth of a man with a machete —

Natalia was through the opening, the opening closing, Rourke hacking it open again with the knife, blasting it open with the remaining rounds in the magazine of his one loaded pistol.

He was through, Natalia looking behind her as she ran — she was loading an M-16, perhaps twenty yards ahead of him.

He ran for her — Natalia shouted, "John — flat on the ground!"

Rourke threw himself forward and down, rolling, gunfire over his head, Natalia's M-16, firing into the wall of attackers as they pursued.

On his back, Rourke dropped his knife, rammed the Colt into his belt, found the M-16—he snatched two spare magazines, both from the musette bag at his left side, buttoning out the spent magazine, letting it be lost, ramming one of the two fresh sticks up the well of the assault rifle, working the bolt release—

He was rolling again, Natalia's rifle empty—

The Gerber in his left fist along with the spare thirty-round stick for the M-16, Rourke was up, pumping the M-16's trigger, cutting down men in waves as they ran from the still burning barricade.

And then Rourke started to run, firing out the stick, dropping the empty to the pavement, ramming the fresh one home, hands reaching for him—he hacked out with the knife, hearing a shriek of pain.

He wheeled, firing point blank into four men, cutting them down.

The nearest of the pursuers was ten yards back—but there were dozens behind this nearest man.

Rourke ran, Natalia running just ahead of him, her M-16 spitting three-round bursts—bright tongues of yellow light in the night—

Rourke's breath was coming in gasps—his M-16 firing behind him, he ran.

Michigan Avenue—Natalia turned right—instinctively, he thought, heading for the lake, for her uncle, despite the KGB, despite the fact that she was wanted — dead.

Rourke was after her, firing out the M-16, dropping out the empty to the sidewalk, Natalia running diagonally across Michigan Avenue, toward the park between Michigan Avenue and the lake, Rourke after, a fresh magazine going up the well of the M-16.

Behind him as he reached the opposite curb — the pursuers had stopped.

"John!"

Natalia's hoarse whisper from the darkness beside a statue.

Rourke ran to her, his stomach aching with the exertion, his breath in short gasps — he coughed, fresh loading the CAR-15 — he had lost three M-16 magazines — but he had plenty more. He had lost one .45 ACP magazine, standard Colt — but it had been an ordinary magazine and was not irreplaceable.

They had burned he didn't know how many hundred rounds of ammo.

"Get that — that — that — the eight hundred-round box — bottom of my pack — strapped there — reload magazines."

He heard Natalia — "Yes." He felt her working at his back to remove the ammo box.

He dropped to his knees beside the statue, both Detonics pistols reloaded, the Colts — all three reloaded as Natalia loaded thirty-round magazines from the box.

He started reloading his .45 magazines — the eight-round Detonics extension magazine, the smaller magazines for the little Detonics pistols —

"What the hell stopped those crazy people?"

"We're in Grant Park," she answered. "The urban Brigands I spoke of — these ones are armed, perhaps as well as we are. And they cut the heads off their victims to show they don't like intruders. I don't know where they live — but between here and the band shell — a no man's land — not even our patrols will go into the park at night unless they have infrared equipment."

Rourke looked at her, feeling sweat drip off his face. He found one of his cigars, chewed down on it, lit it — coughed as the smoke entered his lungs.

"So between us and your uncle — more loonies?"

Natalia nodded, lighting a cigarette. "Yes — more — more of them."

He wondered what they could be like — if the crazy men from the underground were afraid.

"Let's go — right up the middle," he told her.

Chapter Forty-eight

They had left the metal ammo box behind, the remaining cardboard boxes of twenty 5.56mm Ball divided between Rourke's pack and Natalia's — equally.

They moved at a fast commando walk, through the middle of the park.

A bright moon, Rourke could see the trees — dead and leafless. The grass beneath their feet, he knew, was dead too.

The neutron bombing.

They walked on.

"Any idea how we'll get to your uncle — once we get to the museum?"

"The museum guards are army — or at least they were — and they are loyal to my uncle and to me — my uncle would assume, I think, that we can get inside —"

"I hope you're right," Rourke told her softly, walking.

Dead trees flanked them now as briefly they stepped into a paved walkway — the most direct route across the park, if he remembered it correctly. On business in Chicago, he had frequently stayed in Michigan Avenue hotels and walked the park to unwind, to relax. He tried making the memories surface, to guide him.

The noise of a whistle stopped him.

"The Brigands," Natalia whispered.

"No guns unless we have to," Rourke cautioned. They were too close to the hub of Soviet activity and gunfire might bring the whole KGB down on them.

Rourke's right hand went to the big Gerber knife, his left snatching out the black chrome AG Russell Sting IA.

He heard the clicking sound of Natalia opening and closing the Bali-Song—it was advertising— "Don't tread on me,"—and also on her nerves, he thought.

A man shape stepped out of the dead trees into the gray gloom.

"Nice night for a walk in the old park, ain't it?"

Rourke answered him—the voice more New York-sounding than mid-western, Rourke thought. "Yeah—nice and romantic—listening to the whistle of the punks in the trees, the moonlight—whole nine yards."

"You Russians?"

Natalia answered him, "I am Russian—"

"Hey—sexy voice, lady—real sexy—what you look like without your clothes?"

"Yeah—me—I wanna see—right now—" Another figure stepped from the trees.

Then another and another and another, finally perhaps eighteen of the urban Brigands flanking them on both sides, as the trees flanked them.

"You forced this, didn't you," Natalia whispered.

"Better than havin' them stalk us in the park," Rourke smiled.

"If I fire a gun," Natalia shouted, "the entire Russian military will be down on you—I am Major Natalia Anastasia Tiemerovna—the KGB!"

"No shit, woman," one of the figures laughed. "KGB women fuck as good as other women, huh?"

Rourke looked at the figure belonging to the voice. "You open your goddamn mouth one more time, I'll kill you—period."

The figure stepped back a little, silently.

Rourke turned his attention to the figure at the center of the walkway, saying, "We're going past you or over you—your choice, asshole."

"Man—you can't come here into my goddamn park and talk shit to me, man!"

"I just did—asshole."

"You gonna die, sucker!"

Rourke nodded his head, "You bet," and he rasped to Natalia, "cover me, but don't interfere unless you have to—watch yourself."

The two knives in his hands, Rourke started forward—Natalia called softly behind him, "Let me do it—"

She was better with a knife than he was—he knew that. He ignored what she said.

The little Sting IA was palmed in his left hand, invisible in the darkness he hoped—he moved the

Gerber—to draw attention to it, make it the focal point.

Rourke stopped, two yards or so from the man in the center of the walkway.

"Past you or over you?" Rourke asked. "Question still stands." The man wore a gun—some kind of revolver in a shoulder holster over his sweater.

"I oughta shoot you, man," the man challenged.

Rourke shrugged his shoulders. "You're better off with a knife—I'm very good with a knife, so maybe you have a little bit of a chance. With guns, you'd be outclassed. Stick to the knife."

And now the man shouted to his friends, "This sucker thinks he's so good—shit—" he drawled.

"What's your strategy—you gonna bore me to death talkin' or start fighting?"

The man lunged, a switchblade flicking audibly open, the blade catching a glint of moonlight, Rourke feigning with the big Gerber, the man side-stepping, Rourke's left hand punching out, the Sting IA clenched tight in his left fist, the spear-point blade stabbing into the carotid artery on the right side of the neck.

There was a scream, Rourke feeling blood squirt onto his hand as he backstepped, the man going down in a heap.

Rourke stepped back, making the big Gerber disappear into its sheath, his right fist now swinging the M-16 forward, the thumb flicking off the safety.

The men from the trees on both sides were edging in, Rourke stooping to wipe clean his little knife on the dead man's sweater.

Rourke stood up, sheathing the knife.

He took his cigar in his left hand, studying the glowing tip a minute, then replaced it between his teeth.

"This has gotten awful tedious," Rourke called in a loud whisper. "I mean, a real drag. Now fight and die or run and hide—doesn't matter shit to me."

Searchlights lit the ground—from above, Rourke thought, but he wasn't certain.

"Commies," one of the figures shouted, all of them breaking and running, Rourke starting to move.

"Major Tiemerovna!"

The voice, English but Russian-accented, from beyond the edge of the light, down the walkway. "Major! Please—I beg of you, stop—"

Natalia was running, swinging her M-16 toward the lights to fire, Rourke wheeling, in a crouch, the muzzle of his M-16 coming up—

"It is Captain Vladov—major!"

Natalia's voice—

"John—it is all right, I think—he is my uncle's friend—"

Rourke didn't move the rifle's muzzle for an instant, the searchlight going out—its origin was ahead of them, not from above—

The Russian voice again. "I have come to find you—we travel the park here each night in hopes you are coming, major—and this man is Rourke?"

Rourke didn't move his weapon.

"John—" It was Natalia.

Rourke lowered the M-16—thinking it might be the last stupid thing he would ever do.

Chapter Forty-nine

They walked in total silence, in darkness save for the bright moon, through the park. Captain Vladov led the way with his three men, Vladov and his men in black camouflaged-pattern fatigues, their faces and hands blackened as well.

They reached what Rourke recognized as Columbus Drive, the street running parallel to the lakefront and Lake Shore Drive itself. The fountain at the middle of the square now seemed odd — no lights, no water — stillness.

Vladov waited behind bushes near the street, signaling silently to one of his men — the man ran to the curb, then signalling. Vladov whispered hoarsely — "Hurry!"

Vladov ran ahead, Rourke and Natalia running abreast behind him, the two other men following, Rourke recognizing their rifles as the new 5.45 mm AKS 74s — Vladov and his men were paratroopers — he could tell from the stylized berets, and likely the Soviet equivalent of Special Forces.

They halted in dead underbrush — but in the

moonlight Rourke could see sprigs of pale green — new life.

Vladov, a pistol in his right hand — he had carried it since Rourke had first set eyes on him — turned, still crouched, saying, "Your uncle, major — my men and I have been patroling the park each night, a similar patrol on the far side of the museum — he almost despaired, comrade," and the man smiled at her — warmly.

"So had I," she laughed softly. "Almost despaired."

"There's no need to speak in English — I speak Russian," Rourke advised Vladov.

"Very good," Vladov nodded, slipping into Russian then. "The comrade general — he is watched by some of the residual forces of the KGB — but Colonel Rozhdestvenskiy is no longer here — it is rumored he has gone to a place in Colorado called The Womb. Our forces mass for an attack against United States II, but this is senseless commitment of troops — these are your uncle's words, comrade major — there is something afoot."

Rourke studied the man's gun as he listened to him. "What are you doing with a Smith & Wesson automatic and the AKS-74 assault rifle?"

"You are observant, Dr. Rourke — we are the Soviet equivalent of your — " and he said the next two words in English — "Special Forces. Officers are allowed to choose their own personal weapons, and we are all issued the AKS-74 — it is more efficient. Now," and he seemed to dismiss the subject, "we shall make all good speed to the museum — the guard posted at the main entrance is friendly to

221

our cause — but we must hurry," and he rolled back the cuff of his black and dark green night jacket — the watch was a Rolex. "The guard will change in less than forty-five minutes."

"My uncle," Natalia asked. "He is well?"

"The comrade general is well — yes, comrade major," Vladov grinned, adding, "and as tough a man as ever. It will gladden his heart that you are well." And he looked at Rourke, "But we must hurry — there will be no need for shooting — you see, I have looked at your guns."

"I hope you're right," Rourke only told him. And then, Vladov in the lead, they began to run again.

Chapter Fifty

They had reached the main entrance to the museum from the side, by circling behind the structure — and the guard there, a young, florid-faced man who looked very tired, had pretended they were invisible, never acknowledging their presence, never following with his eyes as they had gone up the steps toward the heavy doors.

Vladov used a key — two of the men went through first, the third in a guard position in the shadow beside a pillar at the head of the stone steps.

Vladov was checking his watch — then he said in English, "Hurry — inside." Natalia went through, Rourke behind her, Vladov after them, closing the door as his men came through, then locking it from the inside.

Vladov rasped, "That way — hurry!"

The figures of two fighting mastodons dominated the central hallway, Rourke running past them waved on by the two Special Forces men who had gone through first, toward mezzanine stairways, Natalia taking the stairs three at a time in a run, Rourke behind her, doing the same, Vladov and the third trooper behind him.

At the head of the stairs, the two Soviet SF men waved them down a left-hand corridor, Natalia following, Rourke beside her now, Vladov giving an order in Russian to the third trooper to stand guard by the mezzanine and stay out of sight.

They slowed their run, walking in dark shadows, a golden light ahead of them. The two Soviet SF men turned right into a side chamber, Rourke and Natalia after them—Rourke stopped.

At the far side of the chamber—perhaps some sixty feet away, was a man, huge in his bulk, but of average height and not more. His face was a combination of sternness and the warmth of a homeless dog, his uniform tunic open, his feet moving as though it hurt him to stand.

Natalia ran into his arms, the man seeming to smother her.

"That is Comrade General Varakov," Vladov said with obvious pride. "I am sure that as the friend of the major you will not, but should you attempt to harm the comrade general, I would willingly—even gladly—die in his defense."

Rourke studied Vladov's eyes, saying, "You know—I think you would."

Chapter Fifty-one

They had moved — silently but slowly because of Varakov — Rourke, had circumstances been different, would have liked to have examined the old man's feet to see if perhaps some remedy for the man's obvious pain would suggest itself. They were deep within the museum now, in what was apparently part of an Egyptian wing, glass cases dominating the high-ceilinged chamber, inside the cases ranks of mummies and sarcophagi, and about the hall various items of antiquity of Egyptian origin.

The third Soviet SF-er had rejoined them, and now all three men stood guard at the entrance-ways, Varakov seated on a backless low wooden bench, Natalia huddled beside him — for all the world looking like an overly tall little girl. Rourke smiled.

Rourke stood, and beside him stood Captain Vladov.

General Varakov at last spoke. "There is little time — perhaps no time at all, but only God — if indeed there is one — can determine that now." A woman joined them — slightly built, what most men would call plain, but a prettiness about her. She walked over to stand beside and slightly behind Varakov, the bench separating them.

"Catherine," Natalia murmured.

"Comrade Major Tiemerovna," the woman smiled.

Varakov looked at the woman, her right hand going to rest for a second on his right shoulder, lovingly, Rourke thought, then moving it away, folding it inside her left hand, both hands held in front of her overly long uniform skirt.

Varakov continued to speak, "There is little time. So, very plain talk, Dr. Rourke. Natalia. Captain Vladov. First, Captain Vladov — after our discussion here, unless I am greatly mistaken, my niece and this man, Dr. Rourke — they will be going to Colorado, to The Womb — all is ready for you and your Special Forces to accompany them?"

"Yes, comrade general," Vladov answered.

"What are you talking about?" Rourke asked softly.

Varakov turned to Natalia. "Child — what does ionization of the atmosphere mean to you? You were very bright at the polytechnic — so tell this to me."

"The air — it would become charged with electrical particles — and — "

"When the sun heated it," Rourke interrupted, "the electrically charged particles would — "

Varakov continued to speak, interrupting Rourke. "You are correct — both of you. I had little education — it took me a great deal of time to grasp

226

this idea. But soon, all will understand it."

"You alluded to the end of the world," Rourke whispered.

"In the Judeo-Christian Bible, I believe that God promises this man who built the big ship —"

"Noah," Vladov said.

Varakov looked at him and smiled. "Noah — He promises Noah that the world would never again end by water flooding it over, but by fire instead."

"I always thought that was a poor bargain on Noah's part," Rourke interjected. "I'd rather drown, I think, than burn to death."

"But this will be swift, Dr. Rourke — so swift — so very swift."

"Total ionization of the atmosphere," Rourke murmured.

"Yes — the end of the world. It is coming. Perhaps," and Varakov looked at a rectangular wristwatch that seemed like something out of a 1940s movie or a museum, "in less than five hours, perhaps in another twenty-four hours after that, perhaps a few days. As best the data I have compiled can confirm, the total ionization should be complete within five days at the most — most likely, less than that. It will come at dawn, rolling through the sky, fire, consuming everything, the very air that we breathe, purging the Earth. Each sunrise for twenty-four hours will be the last sunrise, the fire storm sweeping the entire planet. Death for all living things, and should something by some quirk of fate survive, there will be no air to breathe for at least three hundred years afterward, nearer five hundred years before the oxygen content would be able to sustain higher life forms without special breathing apparatus. With this War we fought, this insanity—we have destroyed ourselves—finally and irretrievably, and all mankind shall perish from the Earth forever."

There was nothing John Thomas Rourke could think of to say.

Chapter Fifty-two

John Rourke sat cross-legged on the floor. Natalia had moved from the bench to sit beside him, and she held his hand.

Catherine, Varakov's secretary, Rourke understood, sat beside the general on his wooden bench—the general looked very old.

Varakov held both her hands in his massive left hand.

The old general had kicked off his shoes.

Rourke smoked a cigar, Natalia a cigarette.

Rourke stared at the mummies—his future brothers, he thought absently.

"The Eden Project," Varakov said slowly. "With the ionization would come the complete destruction of breathable atmosphere, at the lowest elevations the air thinner afterward than on the highest mountains. The partial destruction of the ozone layer at the very least. All of this was a postwar scenario, one of many. For a time, it was like a guessing game—this War of Wars. World War III."

"Einstein," Rourke murmured.

"What?"

Rourke looked at the general. "He said something about it once—something like—it was in answer to a question about what would the weapons of world War III be. He told the questioner that he didn't know, but that World War IV would be fought with rocks and clubs."

"World War IV—that is why I have called you here, Dr. Rourke."

Rourke looked at Varakov. "I don't understand, sir."

"You, doctor—your sheer survival, your background—you are like the men in the Russian fairy tales who rode the horses of power and fought evil. My niece—she is consummate in her skills at destruction, yet both of you are human beings, have experienced love—for each other and others. Captain Vladov here—he is, to my reckoning, the finest soldier in the Soviet Army—"

"Comrade general, I—"

Rourke looked at Vladov—the man was embarrassed, but pride gleamed in his eyes again.

"I have found a small cadre of GRU and army personnel whom I can trust. I would advise, perhaps, that you contact U.S. II headquarters through the Resistance—and perhaps they can send forces to aid all of you. Otherwise, the only ones who will survive the last sunrise are two thousand men and women handpicked by Rozhdestvenskiy—ones your husband—" and he looked at Natalia, "had selected, the list only slightly altered after Rozhdestvenskiy took over his position here. One thousand of the KGB Elite Corps, one thousand women from all branches of service, a staff of doctors, scientists, researchers—three thousand in all, perhaps a few less. They will inherit the Earth if you do not act."

"A final act of revenge—I can't see you bringing us here for that," Rourke smiled.

"My letter—to avenge myself on the KGB? Hardly, Dr. Rourke—you are right."

"You mentioned the Eden Project, Uncle Ishmael," Natalia almost whispered.

The old man nodded.

"Postholocaust scenarios—the guessing game, yes." The old man sighed, then continued to speak. "That we would blow away our atmosphere, that we would pitch the planet itself out of orbit and send it hurtling toward the sun, that radiation would blanket the Earth and all living things would die of lingering horror. It is like this boat builder," and Varakov smiled, looking at Captain Vladov, "this Noah. For this is exactly what was built—an Ark. That is the Eden Project, my children, an Ark, and should Rozhdestvenskiy and his KGB Elite Corps survive, they will use the particle beam weapons installed at this womb of theirs—Cheyenne Mountain, your NORAD headquarters before The Night of The War," and he looked at Rourke. "They will use these weapons to destroy the six returning space shuttles five hundred years from now, to destroy the last survivors of the human race except themselves, so they will be masters of the new Earth."

Rourke watched General Varakov's eyes—the light of reason in them, not hatred or jealousy or fear.

It was rare, perhaps once in a lifetime, if that, Rourke thought, that one sat at the feet of greatness, as he did now.

"Your scientists and ours—for many years they attempted, Dr. Rourke, to solve the mysteries of cryogenic sleep for use in deep space travel and exploration. But, independently, both scientific worlds reached the same impasse. The subject could be placed in suspended animation, but if deeply enough to retard the aging process so the cryogenic sleep would be useful, then too deeply for the brain to be revived. It was the scientific establishment of the United States that cracked the right chemical codes and developed a serum which, once injected into the subject artificially, induced the deep sleep of cryogenic freezing before the actual freezing process took hold. This serum allowed what Soviet scientists were unable to do. It allowed the brain wave patterns of the subjects to stay at sufficient level that the subjects could be aroused from their sleep. Otherwise, without the serum, the subject would sleep forever or until the machine that sustained him was disconnected or became too worn to function.

"The Americans," Varakov continued, "had this serum and we did not. Utilizing the pressurized cargo bays of the space shuttles, it was your own Dr. Chambers, your de facto President, who was largely responsible for the plan. With deep space travel within reach, awaiting only technological breakthroughs in propulsion or funding level increases, an international corps of astronaut trainees was assembled, of all races, from all nations of the NATO, SEATO and Pan American Alliances—all nations of the world except the Soviet Union and The Warsaw Pact nations. They were trained arduously—one hundred twenty of the finest and best, the healthiest and brightest, the most skilled and most talented. They were never told their other, possible, secret use."

Varakov stood up and began to pace, Rourke watching the man as he moved—his feet must have been a source of agony, but it was a soldier's disease, Rourke reflected.

"At times of international crisis, what were called Eden Project drills were held, the participants never aware. The space shuttle fleet was manned with its occupants and their gear, the injections given all aboard except the flight crews. They were never launched, until The Night of The War. It was gambled that always five of the six shuttle craft would be on the ground and at least four functionally ready. All six were on the ground, all six ready because of the protracted nature of the crisis. One hundred twenty souls, plus the six, three-man crews. A cargo bay that held microfilm of all the world's greatest learning, greatest literature, sound libraries of music, video libraries detailing medical techniques, construction techniques, cryogenically frozen embryonic animals and fish and birds—an Ark. That is the Eden Project. And," Varakov turned to stare at John Rourke—Rourke watching the man's dark eyes, the sadness there, "these ships were launched before the missiles destroyed the Kennedy Space Center. They cleared our radar—presumably they are out there, on an elliptical orbit that will take them to the very edge of the solar system and then return them to Earth in five hundred and two years. In Colorado, at this moment, Rozhdestvenskiy and his KGB Elite Corps prepare themselves for the cryogenic sleep, to awaken in five hundred years and destroy the Eden Project when it returns. What I offer you, Dr. John Rourke, is the hope that you and your wife and children will survive this final holocaust. Twelve of the American cryogenic sleep chambers were taken from an underground laboratory in Texas. Along with these, dozens of jars—we know not exactly how many—of the cryogenic serum that prevents the brain death of the subject. Go to Colorado, steal back this serum—what you need for your family and yourself and your friend Rubenstein. And for Natalia—I beg that.

"Steal however many of the cryogenic chambers you will need, however many this airtight Retreat Natalia speaks of will support. Save yourself, save Natalia, save your family—perhaps these men as well," and he gestured toward Vladov, the Soviet Special Forces captain. "But above all, lest the devil himself should inherit the Earth, destroy The Womb, rob Rozhdestvenskiy of the cryogenic serum—otherwise," and General Ishmael Varakov sank heavily to the bench, once again holding the girl—Catherine—by the hand, "otherwise, all the light of humanity will be extinguished in evil forever."

John Rourke had no words to speak.

ADVENTURE AND WAR FROM NEL

The Survivalist 1: Total War	*Jerry Ahern*	£1.50
The Survivalist 2: The Nightmare Begins	*Jerry Ahern*	£1.50
The Survivalist 3: The Quest	*Jerry Ahern*	£1.50
The Survivalist 4: The Doomsayer	*Jerry Ahern*	£1.75
The Survivalist 5: The Web	*Jerry Ahern*	£1.50
The Survivalist 6: The Savage Horde	*Jerry Ahern*	£1.50
The Survivalist 7: The Prophet	*Jerry Ahern*	£1.50
Devil's Guard	*George Robert Elford*	£1.95
Kizilkar	*George Robert Elford*	£1.50
Assault Troop 1: Blood Beach	*Ian Harding*	£1.50
Assault Troop 2: Death in the Forest	*Ian Harding*	£1.50
Assault Troop 3: Clash on the Rhine	*Ian Harding*	£1.60
Assault Troop 4: End Run	*Ian Harding*	£1.75
The Zone 1: Hard Target	*James Rouch*	£1.00
The Zone 2: Blind Fire	*James Rouch*	£1.00
The Zone 4: Sky Strike	*James Rouch*	£1.25
The Zone 5: Overkill	*James Rouch*	£1.25

All these books are available at your local bookshop or newsagent, or can be ordered direct from the publisher. Just tick the titles you want and fill in the form below.

Prices and availability subject to change without notice.

NEL BOOKS, P.O. BOX 11, Falmouth, Cornwall

Please send cheque or postal order, and allow the following for postage and packing:

U.K. – 55p for one book plus 22p for the second book and 14p for each additional book ordered to a £1.75 maximum.

B.F.P.O. & EIRE – 55p for the first book plus 22p for the second book and 14p per copy for the next 7 books, 8p per book thereafter.

OTHER OVERSEAS CUSTOMERS – £1.00 for the first book, plus 25p per copy for each additional book.

Name ....

Address ....

....

CRIME AND THRILLERS FROM NEL

Dirty Harry 1: Duel for Cannons	*Dane Hartman*	£1.50
Dirty Harry 2: Death on the Docks	*Dane Hartman*	£1.50
Dirty Harry 3: The Long Death	*Dane Hartman*	£1.25
Dirty Harry 4: Mexico Kill	*Dane Hartman*	£1.25
Dirty Harry 5: Family Skeletons	*Dane Hartman*	£1.25
Dirty Harry 6: City of Blood	*Dane Hartman*	£1.50
The Big Kill	*Mickey Spillane*	£1.50
I, The Jury	*Mickey Spillane*	£1.25
Kiss Me, Deadly	*Mickey Spillane*	£1.50
My Gun is Quick	*Mickey Spillane*	£1.50
The Snake	*Mickey Spillane*	£1.50
The Twisted Thing	*Mickey Spillane*	£1.75
Vengeance is Mine	*Mickey Spillane*	£1.50

All these books are available at your local bookshop or newsagent, or can be ordered direct from the publisher. Just tick the titles you want and fill in the form below.

Prices and availability subject to change without notice.

NEL BOOKS, P.O. BOX 11, Falmouth, Cornwall

Please send cheque or postal order, and allow the following for postage and packing:

U.K. – 55p for one book plus 22p for the second book and 14p for each additional book ordered to a £1.75 maximum.

B.F.P.O. & EIRE – 55p for the first book plus 22p for the second book and 14p per copy for the next 7 books, 8p per book thereafter.

OTHER OVERSEAS CUSTOMERS – £1.00 for the first book, plus 25p per copy for each additional book.

Name ....

Address ....

....

**Give them
the pleasure of choosing**

Book Tokens can be bought
and exchanged at most
bookshops in Great Britain
and Ireland.

NEL BESTSELLERS

Forced Landing	*Thomas Block*	£1.95
The White Plague	*Frank Herbert*	£2.50
No Place to Hide	*Ted Allbeury*	£1.95
It	*Raymond Hawkey*	£1.95
Shrine	*James Herbert*	£2.25
Christine	*Stephen King*	£2.50
Spellbinder	*Harold Robbins*	£2.50
The Longest Day	*Cornelius Ryan*	£1.95
The Case of Lucy B.	*Lawrence Sanders*	£2.50
Acceptable Losses	*Irwin Shaw*	£1.95
The Seven Minutes	*Irving Wallace*	£2.25

All these books are available at your local bookshop or newsagent, or can be ordered direct from the publisher. Just tick the titles you want and fill in the form below.

Prices and availability subject to change without notice.

NEL BOOKS, P.O. BOX 11, Falmouth, Cornwall

Please send cheque or postal order, and allow the following for postage and packing:

U.K. – 55p for one book plus 22p for the second book and 14p for each additional book ordered to a £1.75 maximum.

B.F.P.O. & EIRE – 55p for the first book plus 22p for the second book and 14p per copy for the next 7 books, 8p per book thereafter.

OTHER OVERSEAS CUSTOMERS – £1.00 for the first book, plus 25p per copy for each additional book.

Name ....

Address ....

....